Could she be falling
in love
with the boy next door?

Tom grabbed Megan's hand and spun her under his arm. He pulled her toward him, laid his cheek against hers, pointed their arms forward, and led them in a tango down the beach.

"Dip!" he called, as he bent her over backward toward the waves. Their faces were inches apart. She stared into his blue eyes, transformed now into black pools in the night. This was the same Tom she had known since grade school. The same Tom who had joined her in countless goofy stunts. But somehow, he was also a different Tom.

She wondered what it would be like to kiss him.

LAST FLING

Alison Page

HarperPaperbacks
A Division of HarperCollinsPublishers

DEDICATED TO CINDY SAVAGE

This is a work of fiction. The characters, incidents, and dialogues are products of the author's imagination and are not to be construed as real. Any resemblance to actual events or persons, living or dead, is entirely coincidental.

HarperPaperbacks *A Division of* HarperCollins*Publishers*
10 East 53rd Street, New York, N.Y. 10022

Copyright © 1991 by Daniel Weiss Associates, Inc.
Cover art copyright © 1991 by Daniel Weiss Associates, Inc.

Produced by Daniel Weiss Associates, Inc.
33 West 17th Street, New York, New York 10011.

First printing: May, 1991

Printed in the United States of America

HarperPaperbacks and colophon are trademarks of HarperCollins*Publishers*

10 9 8 7 6 5 4 3 2 1

LAST FLING

Megan Becker bent her knees and dug her toes into the sandy ocean floor. She felt the swell that was building in the great expanse of blue and she pushed off just as the wave lifted her and sent her flying toward the shore.

Arms outstretched, she rode the frothy crest, holding her body stiff and tilting her face toward the blazing Florida sun.

She leaped free of the suction at the end of the wave and ran onto the beach, splattering water all over Gabrielle Danzer and Alyssa Chandler.

"Cut it out!" Gabrielle said. "I'm trying to draw here." She brushed the salty drops off of her sketch pad and flipped her long, dark, French braid back over her shoulder.

1

"I can't help it," Megan said. "I'm excited. It's a brand-new day!"

Alyssa looked up from her book. "We've had several brand-new days since we've been in Coconut Beach on spring break," she reminded her.

"Ah, but this one is different," Megan declared as she dried herself with a neon-pink and black towel that matched her bikini. "I can feel it. Today is the day I'm going to meet the boy of my dreams!"

Gabrielle tilted up the brim of her hat to look at Trevor Jamison, who was sitting a few yards away on the top of the Cabana Banana lifeguard tower. At the same time, Trevor glanced over and smiled at her. As of the night before, Gabrielle and Trevor were definitely a couple.

Megan hid her twinge of envy behind a smile. She was the one who had, accidentally, gotten them together.

A minute later, Dylan McLean, Alyssa's new friend, jogged by carrying his sailboard. He and Alyssa exchanged greetings. As soon as he passed, Alyssa, still smiling, ducked her head and studied her book.

Their "hellos" had looked nonchalant, but Megan knew better.

"Go ahead. Gloat!" Megan said. "So what if the two of you have already beaten me in the boyfriend department. Gabby, you have Trevor; and Alyssa, you have Dylan. What kills me is that you *both* managed to find your guys without even trying!"

"Dylan and I are just friends," Alyssa insisted as she adjusted the clip holding up her auburn hair.

"Right. And I wasn't voted class clown by the Leesville High yearbook staff," Megan scoffed. "Friends don't hang out under the palm trees all night, snuggling in the moonlight."

"They were *friendly* snuggles," Alyssa protested.

"You may have convinced yourself that you're only friends, Alyssa, but *I* don't believe a word of it."

"Is that what you did last night, Alyssa?" Gabrielle asked. "I guess I was really out of it. I fell asleep the minute we got back to the condo."

"I'm not surprised," Alyssa answered. "You had some evening! First, getting seasick. Then, falling overboard and having to be rescued."

"And then, falling in love," Megan teased.

"Hush!" Gabrielle looked up to see if Trevor

had heard. "No one has said anything about love, yet."

Megan laughed. "No, but what else would cause Gabrielle Danzer, of all people, to hang around the lifeguard tower? Two days ago you thought all lifeguards—and for that matter, all boys on the beach—were no-brainers. I just think it's ironic that you fell for the biggest hunk on the beach. And you were the one who didn't want to come to Coconut Beach in the first place!"

Gabrielle smiled. *It's strange how everything happened,* she thought. Before last week, she, Megan, and Alyssa hadn't planned to be roommates, or even friends, for that matter. But one disaster after another had brought them all together.

First, there had been her father's winning a Melziner grant that would take him to Washington, D.C., for a week. Unhappy with the idea of leaving Gabrielle alone in Leesville, he had arranged for her to stay with her Aunt Kate while he was away. Gabrielle had protested spending ten days at a condo in one of the wildest resort towns in Florida, but her father had insisted.

Funny. While my father was all for my going to Coconut Beach, Megan's parents were abso-

lutely against her going! she thought. The Beckers were not at all happy about sending their daughter off to a party town without a chaperone. But only a few days before the start of spring break, Megan crashed her car into Gabrielle's and ruined whatever chance she had had of getting her parents to relent. Mr. Danzer had suggested that Megan stay with his daughter at Kate's. Alyssa had joined their crew midway through the long journey to Coconut Beach, after a major blowup with her fiancé, Brock Jorgensen, left her stranded.

And then Alyssa met Dylan, and I met Trevor . . . Gabrielle blushed.

"Could we talk about Trevor at another time?" Gabrielle whispered. She liked Trevor a lot, but she was still getting used to his other identity. She had met him as a fellow artist, birdwatcher, and bookworm. Until last night on the Cabana Banana boat cruise, she hadn't realized that T. J. the lifeguard, whom all the girls on the beach were drooling over, was also the quiet, sensitive, creative boy she had met as Trevor Jamison.

The shock was still fresh. But it was beginning to wear off. She was sitting within twenty feet of the lifeguard tower, wasn't she? Far enough away not to be labeled a "groupie," and not to interfere with Trevor while he was on duty. But close enough to exchange glances and waves.

"Doesn't it make you jealous that Trevor has so many admirers?" Megan asked. She looked over at his tanned, muscular body and sighed. Girls of every age were draped around his tower, trying to get his attention.

Megan continued. "If he were my guy, I think I'd stake out my territory a little closer and let those other girls know just who he belonged to."

"You sound like something out of a second-rate movie," Gabrielle replied. "Trevor can't help it if half the girls on the beach want to hang out in his shade. He's nice to them, but that's as far as it goes. He told me that a long time ago he made a vow not to get involved with tourists. He's polite, but unavailable."

"But he got involved with you," Megan argued.

"Which just shows how right it is between them," Alyssa said, hoping to stop their brewing argument. "Trevor fell for a tourist and Gabby fell for a hunk. They're about the most unlikely couple around, but sometimes unlikely is what works."

"Besides, I might not be a tourist much longer," Gabrielle mentioned casually.

"What?"

Megan couldn't believe what she was hearing. Gabrielle was the one who hadn't wanted to come to Coconut Beach in the first place. Her father had practically forced her to take this vacation and now she was talking about staying?

"Are you really considering your Aunt Kate's offer to stay here for the summer?" Alyssa asked.

"What offer?" Megan cried. "Have I been left out of *everything*?"

"I mentioned this idea to Trevor and Alyssa when we were at the Blue Moon the other night," Gabrielle explained. "*You* were home nursing your sunburn!"

"Which still looks disgusting, but which does feel a lot better, by the way," Megan informed them.

"Anyway," Gabrielle continued, "Aunt Kate told me that she needs a roommate this summer. She's going to be working extra-long hours at the hospital, and she barely has enough time now to keep her plants watered and the food from molding in the refrigerator. She asked if I had any plans after graduation and I told her that I didn't. She thought I could get a job down here. Lots of the stores need extra help during the tourist season."

"And don't forget, you might sell a lot of paintings at Trevor's mother's consignment shop," Alyssa added. "Your being in Coconut Beach for the summer will be a good chance for you and Trevor to see if you're really meant for each other."

"So you're going to move to Coconut Beach to be with Trevor." Megan sighed. "How romantic! I wish it was me."

"Are you still thinking of stealing Trevor away from Gabby?" Alyssa looked horrified.

"No, silly. I wish it was me planning to spend *my* summer with *my* new boyfriend. There are only a few days left to spring break, and I *still* haven't had my spring fling."

Megan plopped down on her towel and began to slather on sunscreen. Her burn *was* better, but she wasn't taking any chances. After the painful experience of having to put on body makeup to cover her sunburn for the bikini contest two days ago, she had become a reformed, and very cautious, sunbather.

"I thought you had some definite ideas about finding Mr. Right," Alyssa said. "When we were cruising into the harbor last night, didn't you mention something about a scavenger hunt?"

"That's right." Megan reached inside her overflowing beach bag and pulled out the crumpled flyer. "The Billy Bowlegs Scavenger Hunt," she read. "Yes. Now that I've lost T. J. to Gabby, this might be my *last* chance to meet the man of my dreams."

She pulled out her hand mirror and fluffed her quickly drying, blond waves into a semblance of order.

"Don't be so dramatic," Alyssa said. "You're the one who's been attracting boys since we arrived. First Chad and Jason in their BMW . . ."

"Don't remind me. I'll never flirt with a college guy again," Megan vowed.

"Oh, I wouldn't go that far." Gabrielle giggled. "Just don't take a midnight stroll with him on a secluded beach without a backup plan."

"I thought I did a good job of faking appendicitis," Megan protested.

"And you made some miraculous recovery," Alyssa remarked.

Megan shrugged her shoulders. "I suddenly remembered that I had my appendix removed when I was ten."

"Well, they say the third time is the charm," Gabrielle reminded her.

"I hope you're right. After my fiascos with Jason and T.J., I think I'm due for success the third time around," Megan said. "In fact, I've just made a decision. I'm not leaving Coconut Beach until I've fallen in love!"

Gabrielle and Alyssa laughed. Only Megan Becker would make such an outrageous statement.

Suddenly, a shadow fell across the sand in front of them.

Megan squinted up into the bright sunlight.

Silhouetted in front of her stood a tall, well-built guy. The sun coming over his shoulder turned his hair almost gold.

Megan's heart leaped into her throat.

2

"Oh. It's you," she said.

"Thanks a heap!" Tom Hooper answered. "A guy loves to be welcomed with open arms. 'Oh. It's you,'" he mimicked.

Megan affected a pretty pout. Tom grinned and turned to Gabrielle. "Nice suit," he said sincerely. "Black looks good on you."

"It'd better. That's all she wears," Megan interrupted. "I've been trying to get her to branch out in the color department, but so far, I've failed miserably."

Tom ignored Megan and spoke to Alyssa. "Did you hear someone talking?" he asked innocently.

"Okay, Tom," Megan said, smiling up into his sparkling blue eyes. "We were just talking about the fact that our vacation is almost over and

11

about how I haven't met anyone yet. I was hoping you were a handsome stranger coming to sweep me off my feet."

Tom knelt down in front of her. He doffed an imaginary hat and bowed low. "Stranger? No. Handsome? You be the judge," he said modestly. "But, if you want to be swept off your feet, I'd be happy to oblige!"

Before Megan knew what had happened, Tom had scooped her up and was twirling her around in the air.

"Put me down, Tom!" she shrieked.

"No chance. Now I have you where I want you."

Tom started to jog down the beach with Megan pummeling his chest and shoulders with her fists. At one point he stopped and turned back to Gabrielle and Alyssa, who were unsuccessfully trying to control their laughter.

"I'm borrowing Megan for a while," Tom called. "She's needed on the volleyball court."

"Be our guest," Alyssa called back.

Gabrielle waved him on. "Oh, please! Don't let us stop you."

Tom executed another bow, this time almost dropping Megan in the sand. "Later!" he called. Then he took off at a fast clip toward the courts.

The sound of her friends' laughter followed Megan as she bumped along in Tom's arms. *We must look like maniacs,* she thought. This wasn't the first time Tom Hooper had done something crazy. In fact, his name was right there next to hers in the yearbook under the title "Most likely to end up a clown in the circus." No doubt about it, they were great together in front of a crowd.

When they were out of sight of Gabrielle and Alyssa, and still several yards from the volleyball courts, Tom slowed down. Megan stopped beating on him. Her hand lay quietly on his chest. Underneath her palm, she could feel his heart thumping.

Suddenly, his words came back to her. "Handsome? You be the judge."

Megan looked up at his strong profile. His eyelashes were the longest she had ever seen on a guy, or on a girl, for that matter. His tousled, blond hair fell over his forehead in charming disarray. There was just the hint of a roughness on his chin, as if he only had to shave every other day. When he smiled, as he was now, the skin around his eyes crinkled.

Tom looked back at her, their faces only inches apart. He stopped walking and for what

13

seemed like an hour, they just stared at each other.

Megan had the crazy impression that Tom was considering kissing her.

"Well?" he said, his voice a deep rumble in his throat. "What's the verdict?"

He knew she had been studying him. Caught in the act, Megan opted for her usual teasing mode.

"Okay," she admitted with a roll of her eyes and a tilt of her head. "Maybe you're a *little* handsome."

Tom grinned.

"Will you put me down now?" Megan asked.

"Of course," Tom said, making no move to release her. "We're here."

"Are you guys going to smooch all day, or can we get on with the game?" Nat Farrell yelled.

Megan looked around in surprise. She had been so wrapped up in what was happening with Tom that she hadn't noticed where they were. The court was only ten feet away. The game had stopped and everyone was watching them! She could just imagine what this looked like to the gang from school—Tom carrying her slowly across the sand, she gazing adoringly into his eyes . . .

"Put me down, you big oaf!" she ordered, loud enough for the others to hear. She looked over at the group and smiled sweetly. "It's impossible to hire good help these days."

"Fine by me," Tom said. He lifted her above his head. "I've done my weight lifting for the day. Now I'm ready for some volleyball. I'll just . . ."

He bent his knees and prepared to throw her over the net.

"Don't you dare, Thomas Theodore Hooper!" Megan threatened.

"Why not?" he cried. "I'm born to be wild!"

Megan screamed as Tom gave her a little push, then let go of her. She felt herself falling, heard the laughter in the background, saw the sand rushing up to greet her.

Then the breath was knocked out of her as Tom caught her an inch before the ground. He stood her on her feet.

"Oops, I slipped!" he said, flashing her a smile. The boys cheered.

Megan smiled back. She patted the side of his face.

Then she punched him in the stomach. Hard.

"Oops, I slipped!"

Megan spun around and marched into the

game to the cheers of the girls and the boos of the boys.

"Service!" Nat yelled and sent the ball hurtling over the net toward Megan's team's side. Randy Tyler tipped it. Ryan Stevens set it up. Tom ran in just in time to slam it over the net.

Megan smiled. It was a speedy recovery.

After that, there was no time to think. Megan noticed that the other team was made up of the people who had snubbed her since they had all left Leesville for Coconut Beach. They were playing fast and furious—and they were playing to win!

Shannon Dobbler sent the ball flying over the net. "I don't know how you dare to show your face on this beach after what you did," she taunted.

Megan slammed the ball to the back of the opposing team's court. "What did I do?" she asked pleasantly.

"You deserted the cheerleading squad. That's what!" The ball sailed over both their heads and dropped somewhere near the back row.

"I didn't desert the squad. You guys kicked me out! Just because I decided not to stay with

16

you at the Flamingo, that sleazy hotel, you declared me an outcast!"

"Heads up, Meg!" Tom shouted.

Megan turned around just in time to send the ball over the net on the third volley.

"*You* made yourself an outcast when you started hanging around with the Black Widow!" Shannon shouted as she jumped and spiked the ball directly at Megan.

"Gabby is my friend!" Megan yelled as she fell on her stomach to save the point.

"How can you have traitors for friends?" Shannon spat back. "Alyssa Chandler is the cruelest person we know."

"You don't know anything!" Megan shot back.

"She dumps poor Brock practically at the altar and then takes up with that McLean jerk from Ashton High. It's bad enough she broke up with her boyfriend, but to drop him for an archrival is the worst!"

"How would you know? You've never *had* a boyfriend!"

"You've had sixteen!"

"I like to play the field."

"Play it now!" Tom hollered. "The ball's coming to you."

Megan looked up just as Tom set the ball up for a perfect spike. She leaped into the air and raised her arm just as Shannon cried, "And you never *were* a good cheerleader!"

Megan's hand connected with the ball.

The ball connected with Shannon's head.

"I guess you scored that point," Tom said quietly.

Shannon threw herself to the ground, moaning in pain. Members of both teams gathered around. Most of them were laughing.

Shannon was livid.

"You did that deliberately! You were trying to hurt me!" she accused, holding her head.

"Don't be silly, Shannon," Megan said. "How was I supposed to know that you'd move your head right under the ball."

"Oh, so you're saying it's my fault?" Shannon sat up, eyes blazing.

"If the bikini fits," Megan quipped.

Shannon stood up and clenched her fists.

Megan was sure Shannon was going to hit her. She braced herself for the blow.

3

"Game's over," Tom cried. "Last one in the water is a rotten egg!" He grabbed Megan's hand and led the race across the sand to the water. They dove over the breaker together.

Megan struck out toward the open sea with long, sure strokes. She worked with the waves, letting them lift her, and then swimming as hard as she could down the back side. Finally, she stopped and tread water to catch her breath.

Tom surfaced beside her.

"You seem to be making a habit of rescuing me lately," Megan said.

"All in a day's work," Tom replied. "I'll stop, if you want me to."

"No, no. I appreciate it. I *particularly* appreciated it the other day at the bikini contest when

19

I was about to be exposed. If you know what I mean."

"Yeah. One squirt from that hose and the makeup hiding your sunburn would have been history," he said with a laugh.

"And probably my second-place prize, too." Megan giggled. "It's funny how things turn out. I couldn't wait to go on my prize date with T. J. And then I run into Gabby on my date and I find out that T. J. is really Trevor, *Gabby's* new guy!" Megan rolled her eyes. "I'm sure glad we got *that* all straightened out."

"Me, too." Tom shook his head and sprayed salty drops in a circle around him. "Too bad you can't patch things up with Shannon."

"Are you kidding? I was looking forward to decking her. But *you* got in the way!"

"Sorry. It's all my fault anyway. I brought you over to the game to try to get the two of you on speaking terms again. The gang's not the same without you."

"Thanks. But, I don't think we'll ever work out our differences," Megan said. "Even if we did, I don't think there's a real friendship to fall back on."

Tom lay on his back and floated. "I thought all you cheerleaders were tight with each other.

You know, from the vantage point of the student council, the squad seems to have it all—popularity, position, personality. Every girl in the school wants to be a cheerleader."

"Maybe." Megan curled her legs up underneath her and slowly waved her arms just under the surface to see how little she had to do to stay afloat.

"Until last week, staying on Shannon Dobbler's good side was one of the most important things in my life. Now I see that all this time I was dressing and acting according to *her* standards, not mine. Then when the cheerleaders totally dumped me, because I didn't stay at the Flamingo . . ."

"Didn't you tell me that your parents wouldn't let you go unless you had a chaperone? Why didn't you just tell Shannon the truth?"

Megan splashed Tom with a handful of water. "Oh, and what do you think would have happened if I had told her the truth?" she asked. "I would have been the laughingstock of the entire senior class."

Tom splashed her back. "You're supposed to keep them laughing. You're the class clown, remember?"

They had floated closer in toward shore and

now the water was shallow enough to stand. Megan dug in her toes and let Tom have it in the face with a sheet of water.

Tom fell over and came up sputtering. "Why you . . ." he began. He started toward her, but churning her arms like a windmill, Megan didn't give Tom a chance.

Tom held his breath and dove under the water.

Megan felt the tug on her legs and had just enough time to gasp for air before she went under.

A second later, they came up laughing and splashing. Megan forgot all about Shannon, the fight on the volleyball court, and her vow that she would spend every spare minute looking for Mr. Right. She was just having fun.

Suddenly, Tom stopped. "Hold on a sec, Meg. Something is wrong on shore."

"Is this a trick?" she asked.

"No trick," Tom said. "Listen."

Megan cupped her hands around her ears and tried to make out what Trevor was yelling into his bullhorn. There was so much noise from the waves and crowd that the announcement was lost before it could reach them.

Megan looked around and saw that the other

swimmers were clambering out of the water while Trevor continued to shout and wave at those farther out.

A boy swam by them, chopping the water as hard as he could. When he stopped for a breath, Megan called out to him.

"What's going on?" she asked. "What's all the commotion?"

He looked at her, eyes wide with fright.

"SHARK!"

"Where is she?" Alyssa said worriedly. "Shouldn't she be out of the water by now?"

"I don't see her," Gabrielle said as she craned her neck for a better view above the mass of bodies on the crowded beach. "Is Tom with her?"

"Everybody okay?" Dylan asked as he ran up the beach toward them. "Quite a scare, huh? You don't get a shark sighting around here very often."

"Megan isn't back yet," Alyssa told him. "We don't know if she heard Trevor's call."

"I see her," Trevor called down to them from his tower vantage point. "She's okay, and Tom is with her."

"Thank goodness," Gabrielle cried a few minutes later as Megan and Tom joined them.

"What a madhouse!" Megan exclaimed. "It's more likely someone will get trampled on the beach than eaten by a shark."

Trevor stood and lifted his bullhorn to his mouth again. "I repeat. All swimmers please exit the water immediately! This is for your safety!"

"What I want to know," Megan said, "is how anyone could have the nerve to put a resort in a shark-infested area!"

Her friends were too busy scanning the surface of the water to answer her.

"How do they know there actually *is* a shark out there?" Megan continued. "We were just goofing around, and then all of a sudden, everyone was in a panic."

"Shannon and Monica Levitts sounded the alarm," Gabrielle said. "They came running up to Trevor to say they saw a fin coming toward them. I guess Trevor saw it, too, so he called everyone out of the water."

"Wow! I'll bet they were really scared!" For a moment, Megan felt more kindly toward her nemesis. If her quick action had prevented anyone from getting hurt, she couldn't be all bad.

"There it is!" Tom cried, pointing to the slick water just beyond the breakers. "I see the fin!"

A collective gasp rose from the crowd on the beach as the lone dorsal fin cut through the clear water straight toward them.

"This is weird," Trevor said quietly.

"What?" Gabrielle asked.

"Great white sharks don't swim this far south, and the sharks we have down *here* don't swim around with their fins above water. That only happens in the movies. In fact," Trevor said as he adjusted his binoculars, "I've never seen a man-eating . . ."

In the frenzy of the next few seconds it was hard to see what was happening. First, the fin was advancing menacingly closer. Girls screamed and backed away from the surf. Guys picked up large, heavy objects and held them at the ready.

Everyone held their breath.

Then, everyone was laughing.

The shark had grown legs and a snorkel and was stepping out of the water. It was like a scene from a James Bond movie, only Bond had a better body.

The laughing crowd parted to let the prankster through as he flip-flopped his way up the beach toward the tower. He peeled off his mask and pointed to the fake fin strapped to his back.

"Gotcha!" he cried, smirking at his attentive audience. "Had ya goin' there, didn't I?"

"It's Mike Bibbitt!" Alyssa remarked. "It figures."

Shannon and Monica ran up to Mike, and each took possession of one beefy arm. They were giggling hysterically.

"We really fooled you guys!" Shannon said.

"That had to be the best stunt this spring break!" Nat said as he slapped Mike on the back. "Good one, buddy."

"How about a cheer for the Leesville High champs?" Monica shouted. "Give me an 'L'!"

"You! Bibbitt! Come here! I want to talk to you!" Trevor's voice blasted out over the bull-horn.

The cheering stopped as Mike turned to face the lifeguard.

"What's the matter, dude? Can't you take a joke?"

"What you did was hardly a joke, Bibbitt," Trevor answered. "You endangered the lives of everyone on this beach. You caused a panic. Shark or not, someone could have gotten hurt."

Mike grinned at the crowd. "You're the one

who panicked, dude. Any fool could see I wasn't a real shark."

"That's not the point," Trevor explained curtly. "The point is that I'm responsible for the safety of everyone on this beach, including you. I can't afford to take chances. I have to act first and investigate later."

"Whoa, am I supposed to be impressed?" Mike drawled. "Guess you need a little more practice at the lifeguard bit, huh?"

"What a jerk," Gabrielle said angrily. "I hope Trevor fines him or something."

Megan nodded. "Mike doesn't realize that by calling Trevor a fool for mistaking him for a shark, he's also calling everyone else fools."

Trevor sat down and put the bullhorn on the platform next to him. "Let me get this straight," he said with a forced smile. "Your shark stunt was just an attempt to give me more practice as a lifeguard? You wanted to make sure I knew my business? Knew how to enforce all the rules?"

Mike strutted up to the base of the tower. "That's right, dude. Anybody ever tell you that you're an ace with that bullhorn?" he asked sarcastically. "Everyone out of the water!" he mimicked in a high, falsetto voice. "It's for your own safety!"

Trevor stood up again. His face was a mask of fury, but his voice was controlled, even polite. "Did anyone ever tell you that the lifeguard has the right to kick troublemakers off the beach?"

"Ooh! I'm shakin' in my flippers."

"You're outta here!" Trevor said, jerking this thumb in the direction of the boardwalk. "For the rest of spring break!" He sat back down and smiled. Then he added, sweetly, *"Dude!"*

"What?" Shannon shouted. "You can't do that!"

Trevor leaned nonchalantly on one arm of his chair. "I just did. Bibbitt, you have five minutes to pack up your gear and get off the beach!"

"No way. You can't just kick him off the beach," Nat protested. "He has civil rights, you know."

Several other football players joined in the fray, shouting their own reasons for thinking Trevor's action unfair.

"A joke. That's all it was."

"We thought you were one of us, T. J.," a girl said with a pout. Megan recognized her as one of Trevor's most stalwart groupies. "Now we know you're just part of the *establishment.*"

"Was that supposed to be a cut?" Gabrielle asked her friends.

"Well, at least Trevor will have one less admirer to worry about," Alyssa said.

Gabrielle grinned. "Too bad. I'm incredibly sympathetic, of course."

Megan wasn't listening to her friends' exchange. She was starting to get boiling mad at the people who *used* to be her friends.

"Why don't you just do what he told you to do?" she shouted at Mike. "Get off the beach!"

"Because he can't do that!" Shannon yelled, pointing at Trevor. "Mike is our friend. If he goes, the rest of us go. We'll boycott the Cabana Banana and every activity planned for the rest of the break."

"Big deal!" Tom said and Shannon glared at him.

"Who cares?" Megan added. "The beach would be better off without you."

Heads swiveled back and forth between Shannon and her gang, and Trevor and his supporters.

They're waiting for him to back down, Megan realized. *Don't do it, Trevor. Shannon has been the queen of mob rule for too long. She needs to be dethroned.*

Shannon climbed the tower and put her face right in front of Trevor's. "I guess you didn't hear me," she said coldly. "Take back your order or we'll boycott your employer. Remember, if Mike goes, we all go!"

"Fine," Trevor said calmly. "Then you *all* have exactly five minutes to pack up and get off the beach."

"You've asked for it now!" Shannon jumped down from the tower and shook her fist at Trevor. "Just wait until my father hears about this. He'll talk to your boss, and you'll be out of a job before you can say Cabana Banana!"

Trevor looked at his watch. "Four minutes and thirty-seven seconds," he said.

"Come on, Leesville!" Shannon let loose her battle cry, the same one she used when she was trying to whip the spectators into a frenzy during a football game.

"We're not going to let some low-life lifeguard stand in the way of our spring break fun. We demand justice!"

A chant rose from the football players, and then it spread throughout the ranks of Leesville's popular clique.

"Justice—justice—we want justice! Justice—justice—we want justice!"

"Let's go talk to the manager! Let's go call my father! We'll see *who* kicks *whom* off of the beach!" Shannon cried.

As the group began to gather their belongings, Shannon turned to Tom.

"Come on," she ordered.

Megan looked up at Tom. "Go ahead if you want," she said. "I'll understand."

"She'll understand?" Shannon mocked. "That means zip from a loser like her!"

"Sorry, Shannon," Tom replied. "I'm staying with Megan."

The look of rage on Shannon's face did little to improve her already flustered appearance. "Another convert, huh, Megan?" she snarled. "First Gabrielle and Alyssa. And now Tom. Or maybe," she added as she flipped her hair around and made a series of ridiculous faces, "you two are in *luuuuvvv*."

"It's not a matter of love," Tom remarked casually. "It's a matter of right and wrong. Trevor is right and you're wrong. I make it a point of staying on the side of right."

Shannon let out a high-pitched cackle. Then she spun around and marched off, leading her parade of senior sheep.

When they were almost at the boardwalk,

Trevor finally made the announcement everyone was waiting for.

"It's safe to go back in the water!" he called through the bullhorn.

As soon as life on the beach was back to normal, Trevor relaxed in his chair. He reached up and began to massage his temples.

Gabrielle could see that the incident had really bothered Trevor.

"You were great, Trevor," she said sincerely. "Fantastic, even. Cool, calm, and collected. Exactly what the perfect lifeguard should be in an emergency."

Trevor's smile was weak as the others joined Gabrielle in her congratulations.

"Yeah, that Shannon Dobbler has quite a swelled head," Tom remarked. "Every year she gets pushier and more obnoxious."

"And this year she's worse than ever," Megan added. "Maybe she knows her reign is about to end."

"Right. There're only a few more months of high school left," Alyssa said. "She won't be top dog in college. She'll be starting all over, her followers scattered in ninety directions."

"And it won't be as easy to use her father's influence to get what she wants," Megan said.

"You don't think she'd really call him and tell him about what just happened, do you?"

Trevor groaned. "I hope not! I really need this job," he said. "You know, I've been working here for three years, and *every* year, someone pulls a stunt like this."

"Don't worry," Gabrielle said. "Shannon and her father can't get you fired. I mean, this isn't Leesville. It isn't even Georgia. How much power can one man have?"

Megan shrugged her shoulders. "I don't know. The Dobblers are pretty rich, and Mr. Dobbler dabbles in lots of different ventures. Let's just hope one of them isn't the Cabana Banana!"

"I'm sure she wouldn't really try to get you fired," Dylan said quickly. "From what I've heard, Shannon Dobbler is more talk than action."

"I don't know," Megan said slowly. "I just don't know."

"Hey, let's get out of here and let Trevor get back to work," Tom suggested. "I've got to meet Jim and Bob, anyway."

"Right," Megan said. "And I'm off to the arcade. I plan to up my score on skeeball. I can't let Alyssa and Dylan hold the record."

Alyssa looked at Dylan and they both shrugged.

"We're off, too," Dylan said. "We're not sure where, but we're bound for somewhere."

"We'll see you all at the Billy Bowlegs extravaganza this afternoon at three, then," Alyssa said.

"You stay, Gabby," Megan whispered. "Trevor looks as if he could use a little tender loving care."

Gabrielle nodded and watched them all go. Then she turned to look up at Trevor.

"I'm sorry," she said. "I'm sorry that people have to act like such complete fools."

Trevor smiled sadly. He gazed out into the ocean, automatically scanning the waves for swimmers in trouble.

"It's not your fault, Gabby," he said, still keeping his eyes on the waves. "It's spring breakers in general. Stunts like that put everyone on the beach in danger. If a real shark shows up now, do you think I'll be able to get everyone out of the water? Everyone'll think it's another joke.

"Anyone who lives here will tell you that you can't joke about sharks. We have ten to fifteen attacks every year, mostly by black tips and spinners. They patrol the surf zone and attack the surfers who are kicking their feet like crazy and doing their best to look like a school of mullet. Along comes a black tip and chomp! One mangled leg."

"That's terrible," Gabrielle said. "And scary."

"The tourists who come down here don't have a healthy respect for the ocean the way the locals do," Trevor continued. "They don't have any respect for the town, either. They don't care how they leave it or what they do to it while they're here."

Gabrielle leaned against the tower and let the platform shield her eyes against the sun.

"Why do you stay?" she asked. "You're old enough to leave."

"I love it here. Oh, it's hard to explain," Trevor said. "I'm like a lot of the locals. On the one hand, we need the tourists to make our livings, so we appreciate them. But sometimes, we wish they would go home and leave us in peace."

Gabrielle was stung by his words. Did Trevor lump her in with all of the "tourists"?

Trevor must have realized what Gabrielle was thinking, because he looked at her intently for a moment before gazing back out to sea.

"I didn't mean you, Gabby. You're not like the

others. And that makes things more complicated and confusing than ever."

"How so?"

Trevor climbed down off of the tower and walked with Gabrielle down to the water's edge, still keeping his eyes on the water.

"I fell for a tourist girl when I was in junior high," Trevor said. "I fancied myself in love and trailed around after her for the whole week she and her family were down here on vacation. We promised to write every day. You know the routine."

"I take it she didn't write," Gabrielle said softly.

"For a while she did, but then she met someone else and that was that."

"That must have been hard on you," Gabrielle sympathized. "Is that why you made a vow never to get involved with a tourist?"

Trevor nodded. "I don't want you to think it was just that one girl who soured me against all tourists . . ."

"Oh!" Gabrielle's eyes twinkled. "It was *more* than one girl?"

Trevor smiled. "No more for me. But I've watched plenty of my friends get hurt trying to have relationships with tourists."

Gabrielle was silent. She was beginning to see how Trevor had built up his resistance to outsiders over the years.

"And then I met you," he continued. "Now I've done it again. In four more days you'll disappear out of my life."

"Oh." Gabrielle smiled. Trevor didn't know of her plan to spend the summer in Coconut Beach!

She was about to tell him that she had no intention of disappearing from his life when a man approached them.

"T. J.," he said. "Status on the beach?"

"All clear, Mr. D'Angelo."

"I heard about the little problem earlier," Mr. D'Angelo said. "I'd like to speak with you about it in my office."

"Sure," Trevor replied. "I've got a break in about thirty minutes."

"No problem," Mr. D'Angelo said. "I called in Tony to take the rest of your shift today."

"Why?" Trevor asked. Gabrielle could see his body stiffen.

"Is this by any chance the young lady you rescued last night?" Mr. D'Angelo asked, avoiding Trevor's question.

"This is Gabrielle Danzer," Trevor said.

"Gabby, this is Mr. D'Angelo, the manager of the Cabana Banana, and my boss."

"Pleased to meet you," Gabrielle said.

"Likewise," he said with a smile. "Glad you're okay."

Then he turned back to Trevor. "You've had a rough twenty-four hours, T.J. I thought you might like to have the rest of the day off. You could spend it with your new friend."

Trevor looked back up the beach and saw Tony climbing up into the lifeguard tower.

"It seems I don't have a choice," he said softly.

Mr. D'Angelo put his arm around Trevor. "Let's go to my office."

Trevor looked back at Gabrielle. "Wait for me?" he mouthed.

She nodded and smiled. It wouldn't do to show Trevor her worry, but she *was* worried. Very worried. Being called into your boss's office always meant a big problem, no matter how nice your boss seemed.

Gabrielle shivered in spite of the sun. She wondered if Shannon Dobbler was behind Trevor's being called in.

She walked back up the beach to collect her towel and bag. Just as she reached them, a gasp went up from the other sunbathers. Gabrielle scanned the surf, expecting to see a shark, and then she noticed that everyone was pointing to the sky.

A small airplane circled overhead, trailing a long sign.

The big, bold, red letters spelled, "BILLY BOWLEGS IS LANDING! TODAY AT 3:00!"

"I'm so glad to get away from that madhouse," Alyssa said as soon as she and Dylan had cleared the throngs of bathers all still talking excitedly about the shark scare.

"Where were you when—" Dylan commented wryly. "It's typical disaster talk. You know, where were you when the earthquake hit in '86? Where were you when Hurricane Daniel swept the streets of Savannah clean?"

"But this shark scare wasn't even real," Alyssa said. She shook her head. "Sometimes I can't believe I ever hung around with some of Shannon's crowd."

"I'm sure they're not all as mean as Shannon. She's beyond unique. We've even heard stories about her at Ashton. Remember the time that the Leesville football team stole our mascot the day before the Homecoming game, and we found him riding on the queen's float during halftime?"

"I believe Ashton trounced us," she answered. "And I remember that I thought the team deserved it for having abducted that cute little monkey."

"It was the least we could do to avenge Monksie."

"I take it that Shannon Dobbler was the culprit?"

"And a few of her cronies."

Alyssa looked back briefly at the beach. "Her infamy is famous."

"I wouldn't want infamy as my claim to fame!" Dylan laughed.

"Neither would I!"

"Hey, I've got a bold idea," Dylan said. "We don't have to be back at the pier until three o'clock, true?"

"True," Alyssa agreed. "What do you have in mind?"

"We've been hanging around the beach for almost the entire week. In fact, in all the times I've come down to Florida, I've never once left the beach scene."

"And what bold thing are you suggesting we do?" Alyssa prompted, savoring the delicious feel of doing something unexpected. For the past four years her life with Brock had been so routine. Dylan was a surprise a minute and she loved it.

"Let's jump on a bus and see where it takes us. We'll get off somewhere and then catch another bus back. What do you say?"

"I've always wanted to travel," Alyssa replied dryly.

"Then, c'mon. We'll start with a trip across town."

Alyssa had never spent a more relaxing or more enlightening day. Escaping the possibility of running into Brock and Jenny made her feel like a totally different person. With each mile the bus took them away from the ocean, Alyssa felt more free.

Soon the landscape changed from palm trees and sand to farms and fields of crops. White, puffy clouds danced in a perfect, blue sky. If she were a painter, like Gabrielle, she thought, surely this sky would inspire her to put brush to canvas.

Alyssa's eyes lit up when the bus came to stop in front of an old, brick schoolhouse. Alyssa glimpsed an overgrown cemetery and an ivy-covered church behind the building.

"Let's get off here," she suggested.

Dylan reached up and pulled the cord again, and the driver waited for them to walk to the front.

"Does a bus come by here to go back into town?" Dylan asked the driver.

"Every hour on the quarter," he answered.

"Thanks," Alyssa and Dylan said together as they hopped off the bus.

Hand in hand they walked up to the schoolhouse and peeked through the dusty windows.

A man working in the garden encouraged them to go inside. "We'll be fixing it up to be a museum soon, but today you can tour for free."

Alyssa smiled at Dylan. "Old things fascinate me," she said. "These bricks are lovely. And look at the mortar between them. It looks like dried mud and sand. I wonder how old the building is?"

Dylan pointed to a tarnished plaque above the door. "Martha Oaks School. Established in 1887," he read.

"Wow," Alyssa exclaimed as they walked inside. "These must be the original desks, the original books, and here's the original woodstove!"

Dylan and Alyssa explored everything in the schoolhouse, including the lard buckets in which the children had carried their lunches to school. Then they walked out behind to view the outhouse, the woodshed, the tiny church, and finally, the cemetery.

"I'll bet tourists never see this side of Coconut Beach," Dylan said. "They stay where all the action is and miss all the charm."

"I like the history of a place much more than the neon lights it's acquired," Alyssa said. "I'd like to visit towns all over the world and learn about the events in their past that shaped their present."

"Have you thought about being an archaeologist or an anthropologist or an historian?" Dylan asked.

"Until this week, I was going to become a legal secretary," Alyssa said with a short laugh. "Brock is planning to become a lawyer and we, I mean he, thought it would be nice if we worked together. My parents, of course, thought it was a brilliant plan, and a good way for us to pay our bills until Brock could set up his own practice."

Dylan ran his hand along the top of an ornately carved gravestone. "Very neat and tidy, as were all of the plans they made for you. What are you going to do now?" he asked.

"I don't know." Alyssa opened her arms wide. "I *do* know that I don't want to live my life as anyone's sidekick. I want to come first in someone's life, not second."

"You're at the top of my list, Alyssa," Dylan said, his voice barely above a whisper.

Alyssa turned away and tried to read the name on one of the worn markers. But the carved letters blurred. These people, dead so long ago, had once had hopes and dreams just like she had now. She wondered how many had been afraid to risk new ventures, and how many had ever thrown caution to the wind and simply followed their hearts.

"I'm scared, Dylan," Alyssa said, letting her tears fall. She walked over to a stone bench and sat down. Dylan sat beside her, but didn't attempt to hold her or to take her hand.

"Of what?"

"Of change, I guess," Alyssa said. "I'm scared of making mistakes. I'm scared of taking risks."

"Everyone makes mistakes," Dylan said quietly. "And you don't reap any rewards if you don't take a risk or two. Besides, I think you *are* a risk taker. Hey, you tried wind surfing, didn't you? And it took plenty of guts to tell Brock to get lost."

"I guess so."

Alyssa leaned her head on Dylan's shoulder and took a deep breath. The air was filled with a sweet aroma. Spring had blanketed the old graveyard with a profusion of colorful wild-flowers. Alyssa thought the color and the disorder was prettier than any pot of plastic flowers or any well-manicured lawn.

"Are you afraid of me?" Dylan asked finally.

"Actually, I'm more afraid of me. I'm afraid that all of the things I once thought were true about myself aren't true anymore. And I'm afraid that if we stay together, we're in for a rocky road."

Dylan reached up to rub the tension out of her neck and shoulders. "I know you want us to go slowly," he said. "But I want to tell you how I feel."

"Hear me out," he added when Alyssa put her finger on his lips to stop him.

"Okay."

Dylan paced in front of her. "I know we're facing some problems ahead. I know all about the statistics on relationships started on the re-bound."

Dylan sat down beside her again. "But, I'd really like to give our relationship a chance. I don't want to give up before we even try. I've never felt this way about anyone before. Talk about being scared!" Dylan laughed. "I could write the book!"

Alyssa curled up her knees and wrapped her arms around them. "I've been fighting with myself ever since I met you," she said quietly. "Part of me knows how right we are together. Meeting you and starting to become my own person has made me realize how shallow my relationship with Brock was. I *do* want to keep seeing you. I *do* want to explore these new feelings. But part of me wants to deny the feelings and to push you away because liking you doesn't feel safe."

"It feels risky," Dylan agreed. "But *I'm* willing to take the risk."

Alyssa sighed. "Me, too," she said. "I just don't guarantee to be logical and together all of the time."

"I don't expect you to be anything but yourself," Dylan answered. "As long as you'll cut me a little slack for all of the mistakes I'm planning to make, too."

Alyssa's smile of encouragement was all the

answer Dylan needed. Coconut Beach and all of the crazy things that had happened to them since they'd been there seemed very far away at that moment.

Dylan kissed Alyssa. His touch was brief and soft and held a promise for the future.

6

Despite their side trip to the old schoolhouse, Alyssa and Dylan were the first to arrive at the pier that afternoon. Megan showed up a few minutes later, full of stories of her day spent sipping sodas at the Paradise Café and checking out the guys at the arcade.

"Pretty elaborate, huh?" Megan commented as they found a good vantage spot near the front of the crowd.

Gabrielle joined them just as the festivities began. All eyes turned seaward as an elaborate pirate ship sailed into view. It docked with much musical fanfare, and costumed pirates leapt out onto the pier.

The pirates in their colorful garb lined up and sang a rousing pirate ditty. As the crowd looked on, each pirate in turn broke from the line and did a series of tumbling moves across the pier.

"Look at those costumes! That wooden leg looks so *real*," Megan cried.

"It can't be real," Gabrielle remarked. "How could he do cartwheels with a wooden leg?"

"Practice, I guess," Dylan said with a laugh.

"This Billy Bowlegs thing must be a major local event." Alyssa turned to Dylan. "Is this an annual contest?"

Dylan ran his hand through his wavy brown hair. "The town's had a Billy Bowlegs Scavenger Hunt every year for at least as long as I've been coming down here on spring break. It's sponsored by WBCH, Beach Rock Radio, and the local merchants. The entry fees are donated to charity."

"Gabby, weren't you saying something the other day about Billy Bowlegs? Wasn't he a famous pirate who used Coconut Beach as his base of operations?" Megan asked. "Like, he founded the town or something?"

Gabrielle looked up at the flapping skull and crossbones that flew from the mast in the center of an authentic crow's nest. "Right. Trevor told me the whole story. Billy Bowlegs is the unofficial 'father' of Coconut Beach. When he was alive, the citizens protested his influence and pretended they were going to bring him to justice one day. But no one complained when he was able to bring supplies to the town during the months of the British blockade, when normal shipping channels were closed."

"So he was kind of a local hero and villain at the same time," Alyssa said. "I think sailing off to faraway places is so romantic! I don't even think I would mind working on the ship for my passage."

"Pirate ships weren't the cleanest places in the world," Gabrielle reminded her.

"No." Alyssa sighed. "But Tahiti, the Bahamas, Tonga . . . sandy beaches, cruising on the high seas with only the stars to guide you, searching for buried treasure . . ."

"Speaking of buried treasure," Dylan said, "supposedly old Billy Bowlegs buried several chests of treasure here in Coconut Beach. No one has ever found them, though. I think it's a legend. You know, just part of the pirate mystique."

"Has anyone ever really *looked*?" Megan asked excitedly. "We could borrow a couple of shovels from Gabby's Aunt Kate and do a little digging after dark."

"You're crazy," Alyssa said with a laugh.

"No. Just broke. What does the winning team in this scavenger hunt get?"

Dylan pointed to a small ornate chest sitting on top of a lace-draped barrel. "The winning team receives all the gift certificates in that chest. I heard that the value is over one thousand dollars this year."

"But what does the team have to do? Just collect all the items on a list, like in a regular scavenger hunt?"

"That sounds easy enough," Gabrielle said.

Dylan rubbed his chin. "It's not as easy as it sounds. You have only six hours to scrounge up a really wild list of items. The organizers spend all year coming up with the craziest, most difficult lists imaginable. No two teams have the same list, but some lists have some of the same items . . ."

"So you could be competing with another team for a particular item, but you don't know which one that might be?" Alyssa asked.

"Exactly," Dylan said. "Not only that, you're competing with teams that have been entering the contest for years. They start preparing months in advance, studying maps of the city and lists of products sold or manufactured at

53

each address, in order to get an edge in the competition."

"Can we still enter?" Megan asked.

"Yes, you can, young lady," a handsome pirate told her. He handed her a registration form and smiled to show a row of perfect, gold teeth. The eye not covered with the black patch winked at her.

Megan winked back. Her eyes followed him as he moved amid the crowd, passing out registration forms. Megan thought he looked rather dashing in his tattered pants and bright green-and-purple striped hose. And that patch over his left eye was very mysterious, very alluring, very . . .

"It's a waste of money," Dylan said. "You'd be going up against practiced hunters with years of experience."

"Read it anyway, Megan," Alyssa urged.

"Megan?" Gabrielle prompted. "I think she's off in Never Never Land. Snap out of it, Meg, and read the instructions."

"Sorry," Megan said as she pulled her attention back to her friends. "I was just trying to imagine what that guy looked like without his . . . uh . . . eyepatch."

"Will you get boys off of your mind for *one* minute."

"I can't help it," Megan complained. "I only have a few more days to find the man of my dreams." Megan quickly scanned the registration form. "It says just what Dylan told us. The scavenger hunt is sponsored by WBCH and the local merchants. The prize chest is worth one thousand-plus dollars and the entry fee is . . . let me see . . . twenty-five dollars for each group, which must be composed of six people."

"When do you have to sign up by?" Gabrielle asked.

"You just show up with your team at two o'clock on Saturday afternoon—an hour before the hunt begins—pay your fee, and get your list. It's easy."

"You're not seriously thinking of entering, are you?" Dylan asked. "You know, even if you're back first with your list, you don't even win the chest outright. Each of the teams that collects everything on its list within the six hours is entered in a drawing for the grand prize."

"Don't be such a spoilsport," Megan teased. "This could be fun. So what if some teams have more experience? So what if they've been working on the hunt for months? *We* have an advantage no other team has."

"We do?" Dylan asked.

"We do. We have Trevor. He knows the area better than any of us."

"But Trevor might have to work," Gabrielle reminded her.

"He could still give us some pointers," Megan insisted. "And I'm sure we could recruit a good-looking guy in his place."

"Ah, so that's it," Gabrielle accused playfully. "You just think this is a good way to meet a guy."

Megan tossed her hair over one shoulder and smiled. "That's not it at all. I'm much more concerned with cooperation and team spirit. I just want us to have another great memory of our stay in Coconut Beach."

"I already *have* a great memory," Gabrielle said softly.

"Speaking of Trevor," Megan said, "how was he doing after we left the beach this afternoon? He seemed pretty upset."

"He was. I told you that his father died. His mom works really hard but she doesn't make a lot of money. His job is *really* important to him. He's trying to save up money to go to college, you know. And then some jerks try to ruin everything for him!"

"Mike Bibbitt certainly falls into the jerk category," Alyssa said dryly. "He and Nat Farrell have absolutely no concept of manners or decency. They live to eat and play practical jokes. And Brock wasn't much better. Night after night Brock would show up late for a date because he had been off whooping it up with Nat and Mike."

"No," Megan agreed, "consideration for others doesn't fit into their game plan. And Shannon's the worst! I hope Trevor isn't worried about her threat to get him fired."

Gabrielle sighed. "He can't *help* but be worried. After you guys left, his boss, Mr. D'Angelo, called him into his office for a talk and told him to take the rest of the day off."

"Did he say it was because of Shannon's complaint?" Alyssa asked.

"Trevor didn't say much when he came out of Mr. D'Angelo's office except that his boss had suggested he might need a rest after the incident on the Banana boat last night and the shark scare today. I'm afraid that means they're trying to let him down easy."

"That's really stupid," Megan said. "How could the management listen to Shannon's accusations? *She* was clearly the one at fault."

Gabrielle shook her head. "I don't know. I guess throwing someone off of the beach is a pretty serious action. Trevor said that Mr. D'Angelo agreed with him . . ."

"But . . . ?" Alyssa asked.

"I'm just worried, that's all. I mean, if he agreed with Trevor's decision, why would he have pulled him off of the beach?"

"Where's Trevor now?" Dylan asked.

"He said his mom has been needing help putting up some heavy shelving units," Gabrielle told them. "I think he just wanted to be alone and sweat off a little of his frustration."

"Makes sense to me," Dylan said.

"So, what about this Billy Bowlegs Scavenger Hunt?" Megan asked impatiently. "I think we should enter."

"But where are we going to come up with the entry fee?" Gabrielle asked.

"I'll think of something," Megan declared confidently.

Gabrielle shrugged her shoulders. "You usually do. In the meantime, let *me* hold the registration form! I don't trust you not to lose it!"

The crowd was beginning to break up and groups of potential contestants began to chat about their strategies as they left. The pirates climbed back aboard their sailing ship and the pirate with the eyepatch waved at Megan.

"Let's go back to the condo and talk strategy," Megan said as she waved back. As she turned to her friends, she bumped into Shannon Dobbler and Monica Levitts.

"Joining the hunt?" Shannon asked with a sly grin. "You don't have a chance!"

"And why is that?" Megan demanded.

"Because," Shannon proclaimed. *"I've* formed a team and *we're* going to win!"

"Says who?" Alyssa asked angrily.

"Says *her*!" Monica answered, jerking her thumb in Shannon's direction. "We have Nat, Mike, Brock, and Jenny on our team. *And* the help of Shannon's father."

"I'm getting tired of your throwing your father's name in our faces," Megan said. "What could he *possibly* know about Coconut Beach? Is he planning to lend you his limo for the hunt?" she added sarcastically.

"A lot you know!" Monica retorted. "Mr. Dobbler has friends in high places, *including* the Cabana Banana!"

Gabrielle put her hand over her mouth to stifle a gasp.

"That's right!" Shannon said smugly. "The Cabana Banana. Where your boyfriend *used* to work!"

Megan and her friends turned and silently walked away. When they were off the pier and down on the beach again, Megan exploded.

"We *have* to enter the scavenger hunt, now," she declared. "If for no other reason than to beat Shannon."

"I absolutely agree," Alyssa said. "It's time Shannon was shown up, once and for all. You heard what Monica said. They're going to use Mr. Dobbler's influence somehow to cheat."

"He'll probably get their list for them beforehand so that they have a head start," Megan predicted. "But *we* have to find a way to beat them at their own game."

"Without cheating," Alyssa added. "Are you with us, Dylan?"

"Are you sure you're not just interested because Brock is on their team?" Dylan asked quietly.

Alyssa shook her head. "Nope. It didn't bother me a bit that Shannon linked his name with Jenny's. I guess I really *don't* care about him anymore."

"I think she means it!" Megan thumped Alyssa on the back. "I think she really means it."

Alyssa turned to Dylan, threw her arms around his neck, and gave him a big kiss on the cheek. "So, are you in or are you out?"

"It's worth a shot," he said, grinning broadly. "By the way, I was very proud of you guys back there. You were in such control, just walking away like that. I don't even *know* Shannon and I felt like slugging her."

"Oh, I felt the same way," Megan said with a shrug. "I just didn't want to hurt my hand."

"And be sued by the Dobblers' sixteen lawyers," Alyssa said.

"What about you, Gabby?" Megan asked. "Don't you feel like wiping that smug look off of Shannon's face once and for all?"

A frown creased Gabrielle's brow. "I'm going to go find Trevor," she said. She turned and ran back toward the pier.

"Tell him we need him," Megan called after her. "We need him on our team if we're going to beat Shannon!"

Gabrielle waved her hand over her head but didn't stop to turn around or answer. She had to find Trevor. *Fired!* He was probably devastated.

Gabrielle jogged back along the pier and out toward Maggie Jamison's shop. When she reached the shop, she burst through the door. "Maggie, where's Trevor?" she asked excitedly.

"He got a phone call a little while ago and left without a word," Maggie answered. "What's going on, Gabby?"

"I think Trevor has been fired."

"Oh, no! Is it because of that girl he mentioned? The one who orchestrated the shark stunt on the beach?"

"Her family is very rich and very powerful. She *always* gets her way," Gabrielle said bitterly. "Whether her way is right or not."

"Check with Trevor's Uncle Steve," Maggie suggested. "Since his father died, Trevor has always gone to my brother when he needs someone to talk to."

"What about Isla de los Pájaros Libres?" Gabrielle asked. "He told me the island was his special hideaway."

Maggie walked over to the back window of her shop and looked out. "No, his boat is still tied up. Check with Steve, first. If he's not there, I guess we'll just have to wait until he shows up."

"Thanks, Maggie. If he comes back, will you tell him I'm looking for him?"

"Sure. Good luck!"

Gabrielle hurried back to the condo, grabbed her keys, and hurried to the garage to get her Mustang. The engine purred when she turned the key. Gabrielle sighed with relief. She hadn't driven the Mustang since she had picked it up from the repair shop. There hadn't been a need. She had been able to get around Coconut Beach by walking.

But she needed the Mustang to get out to the working dock quickly. She remembered the way from the night she and Trevor had ended up on the deck of his uncle's fishing boat, cuddled under a blanket, drinking coffee, and watching the stars.

Please be there, she wished as she negotiated the narrow residential streets. Finally, she reached the parking area for the dock and pulled up between two huge stacks of shrimp traps. Quickly she got out, locked the car, and started to run again.

Please be there.

Then she saw him. His shirt was tied around his waist and his back was covered with beads of sweat. He was lifting a huge crate of fish and heaving it onto a waiting dolly.

"Trevor?" Gabrielle said softly as she came up behind him.

"Gabby." Trevor turned to face her. He wiped his arm across his forehead. "What are you doing here?"

"Is it true?" she asked. She could feel the tears sting her eyes. "Did Shannon have you fired?"

"It's true, all right." Trevor loaded the last crate and then approached her.

Gabrielle noticed the hard lines around his eyes and mouth.

"I'm sorry," Gabrielle said, reaching out to take his hands in hers. "It's so unfair."

"You're telling me! One minute Mr. D'Angelo is telling me how well I handled the situation, and an hour later he calls me on the phone to say that I'm fired. He's sympathetic, but there's nothing he can do. The order came down from the owners."

"Friends of Shannon's father, no doubt," Gabrielle said angrily.

"I wasn't even allowed the chance to tell my

65

side of the story. They listened only to her and . . ."

"She lied," Gabrielle finished for him.

Trevor nodded. "She told them that I had been abusing my authority, pushing people around. According to Shannon, I threw Mike off the beach because we were fighting over a girl."

"What?" Gabrielle exclaimed. "There are at least a hundred witnesses who will testify otherwise."

"Aw, what's the use? She'll just find a way to pay them off." Trevor slumped down onto a pile of rope and Gabrielle sat beside him.

"Can't you get another lifeguarding job somewhere? You're certified by the city, so you're qualified to work on any public or private beach."

"Here's the clincher." Trevor slammed his fist into his hand. "My certificate has been revoked for one month."

Gabrielle gasped. "How did she do that?"

"I don't know, but she did. All I did was kick her pal off of the beach, and now she's trying to ruin my life. She's doing a pretty good job of it, too."

They sat silently for a long while, holding hands and watching the activity on the dock.

"I know it's not much, but I have an idea that might cheer you up a bit," Gabrielle said finally.

"I could use some good ideas right now."

"Megan, Alyssa, and I have decided to enter the Billy Bowlegs Scavenger Hunt. We want you to join us."

"I have to start looking for another job," Trevor said. He shook his head. "College starts in the fall."

"You could take a few hours off to help us win the hunt on Saturday. We need your local expertise," Gabrielle said. "And, it would be a good way to get back at Shannon."

"How?" Trevor asked.

"She told us her father is going to help her win the hunt," Gabrielle told him. "We think she has a way to get a copy of her list ahead of time."

"Is there no end to that girl's gall?" Trevor stood up and began to pace.

"She thinks the world revolves around her," Gabrielle said. "We can't let her win this battle without a fight!"

Trevor turned, pulled Gabrielle to her feet,

and swung her around. "No way! I have a little influence of my own in this town. When the judges hear what she's planning, they'll be furious."

"Do you think they would kick her out of the contest?"

"No. She'd probably have her father cancel the scavenger hunt and wreck things for everyone. But the committee can make sure she has a brand-new list on the day of the contest."

"Then we'll beat her fair and square," Gabrielle said.

"Fair and square. Ha!" Trevor laughed. "I'll enjoy putting those words into Shannon Dobbler's vocabulary."

8

"Who are we going to get to be the sixth member of our team?" Megan asked with a pout.

It was hard not to feel sorry for herself. Here she was, all alone with two happy couples. It was ridiculous. Of the three girls, *she* was supposed to be the boy expert.

The friends had gathered that evening at Dune Buggies, the hottest music and dance club on the boardwalk, to talk about the Billy Bowlegs Scavenger Hunt and to recruit another member for their team.

The trouble was, Megan seemed to be the only one interested in finding the last member. When the two couples weren't clinging together on the dance floor, they were totally wrapped up in each other at the table.

"Let's ask Aunt Kate," Alyssa suggested as she gazed dreamily into Dylan's eyes.

"Kate has to work double shifts at the hospital this weekend," Gabrielle informed them.

"We haven't seen much of your aunt this whole week," Alyssa commented.

"I know." Gabrielle leaned over to sip through one of the straws in the soda she was sharing with Trevor. "She told me this morning that she wished she had more time to spend with us. But they're shorthanded, and she *is* the director of nursing at Centennial."

"We're off the subject again," Megan snapped.

"What subject was that?" Dylan swooped in to steal a kiss from Alyssa.

Trevor leaned down to sip from his soda. His nose touched Gabrielle's and they giggled.

Megan stood up abruptly. "I give up!"

Her friends looked up in surprise, lovey-dovey grins plastered on their faces.

"I'll just have to find someone myself!"

"I think that's a good idea," Alyssa said. "Hey, Dylan. Let's dance."

Megan put her hands on her hips and watched them go.

"What about Tom?" Gabrielle asked gently. "I'm sure he'd join our team."

"Except that he's probably already committed to the student council team," Megan said with a sigh. "I heard that they were all entering together and there *are* only six of them here in Coconut Beach."

"Well, I'm sure you'll have no trouble convincing someone to join us. Just go out and grab the first unattached guy you see. You're good at that."

"Is that a joke?"

"No, it's the truth. I've never told you, but I've always admired the way you jump right into things. You crack a couple of jokes, and suddenly you're the life of the party," Gabrielle said. "Why are you so hesitant now?"

"I don't know," Megan said. She sat down again and rested her elbows on the table, her chin in her hands. "I think because before tonight I was just playing games. Now I'm serious. I really *would* like to find my own special guy."

"You'll find him," Trevor said confidently. "Look at Gabby and me. Miracles do happen."

Gabrielle gave her the thumbs-up sign. "Go for it, Becker!"

71

"All right." Megan stood up again and straightened her shoulders. She really didn't feel so sure of herself, but she knew there was no point in letting her friends in on the secret. "Before this evening is over, I'll have a third guy for our team. And he'll be cute," she added over her shoulder as she headed across the dance floor.

Megan dodged the dancing couples and marched boldly up to the first table of guys she saw.

"Any of you guys free to be my partner in the scavenger hunt on Saturday?" she asked.

"Are you planning on having any more emergencies?" asked a guy with his back to her.

"Jason!" Megan cried as he swiveled around in his chair to face her. *Why couldn't I have checked out this table before I approached them?* she thought frantically. "I'm feeling much better now, thanks to you," she lied. Megan turned her smile on the other fraternity brothers seated at the table. "Jason saved me from a bad case of indigestion the other night."

"I thought you said it was your appendix," Jason said suspiciously.

"How was I supposed to know what it was?" Megan replied. "I'm not a doctor. But the woman I'm staying with is a nurse and *she* told me it was indigestion. And she said you brought me home just in time."

The guys around the table laughed.

"Hey, Jason! We didn't know you had a noble bone in your body," Chad said.

"I can be a gentleman, occasionally," Jason said with a smirk. "For the right 'gentle' lady," he added as he pulled Megan down in his lap.

Whoops and whistles went up from the group.

This is getting out of hand—again, Megan thought.

"I might be willing to abandon my teammates here and join up with you," Jason said, nuzzling her ear. "For the right price."

How did she get herself into these messes? Hadn't she vowed never to get involved with a college guy again unless she had an escape route planned out ahead of time?

Megan smiled slyly and thought fast.

"Yeah," Chad added. "But the rest of us will be *so sad* if you take Jason away. We'll have to be compensated for his loss."

Megan tried to get up but Jason had a firm grip on her waist. The other boys at the table laughed at her dilemma.

"Maybe y'all should be paying me to take Jason off your hands?" Megan joked weakly.

"One at a time? Or all at once?" Chad asked quickly. He licked his lips elaborately.

Megan felt both incredibly foolish and incredibly scared at the same time. She was trapped, and once again, she had brought it on herself. Now, unless she screamed or made a big scene, these guys were going to hold her there all night, making crude suggestions and probably trying to follow through with them, too.

Suddenly, Jason lifted her and stood her on the chair next to him.

"We want to get a good look at our prize," he said.

Megan felt like a cheap doll standing on that chair, being ogled by these fraternity boys. She had to escape and there was only one way to do it. It wouldn't be dignified, but she was going to count to three, leap off the chair, and run as fast as she could for home.

She just hoped they wouldn't follow her.

She closed her eyes.

One (here it comes, humiliation) . . . two (I'll never, never, never flirt again my entire life) . . .

Before she reached three, Megan felt someone jump up on the chair next to her. She opened her eyes to find Tom Hooper grinning down at her.

"Megan, Megan, Megan. I've got to hand it to you. I didn't think you'd pull it off, but you did."

Megan was sure she looked as confused as the frat boys, but she grabbed Tom's arm and held on for dear life. Her smile frozen, she begged him with her eyes to get her out of there.

Tom addressed the nearby tables and the boys in front of them. "Megan bet me fifty dollars that within three minutes she could have an entire table of boys at her feet. And she did it." He looked at his watch. "In exactly two minutes and forty-seven seconds!"

Tom helped Megan down off the chair. "Congratulations!" he said. "And thanks for being such good sports, guys." Tom looked around the room. "Let's give them a big hand, shall we?"

While the people at the tables around them were laughing and clapping, Tom propelled Megan through the crowd and out the door.

It wasn't until they were outside in the cool, misty, evening air that Megan let out her breath in one big sigh.

"My knight in shining armor," she said as she gave Tom a hug.

She started to pull away and say something funny about damsels in distress, but Tom held her tight. "It's okay, Meg. You don't have to pretend with me."

Megan burst into tears. "Will I ever learn?" she sobbed. "Why does my personality work back in Leesville but not here? Back home, the kids can take a joke. They know that flirting is a harmless game."

"College guys are different. They've lived on their own and have different expectations. If you promise something, they expect you to deliver."

"Did you hear the whole thing?" Megan asked.

"Enough to know that you were in trouble."

Megan cried even harder. "If you hadn't come along when you did . . ."

"Hush," Tom said. "It's over now."

They stood quietly for a few moments until Megan brought her tears under control. She didn't make any move to separate herself from the warmth of Tom's embrace.

Around them a light rain began to fall but Megan felt comfortable and protected.

"It's raining," Tom said as he brushed her hair back from her face.

"I know."

"Do you want to go back inside?"

"No."

They began to walk, their arms still around each other. When they reached the sand, they kicked off their shoes and waded out into the dark water.

As they walked along it crossed Megan's mind that what she needed to do was to find a boyfriend like Tom. Someone who understood her crazy moods and her somber ones. Someone who enjoyed walking on the beach in a drizzle and who didn't expect anything of her. For the first time Megan realized that the woman who finally caught Tom Hooper was going to be one very lucky person.

"I was really stupid back at Dune Buggies," she confided after a while.

"We all do stupid things," Tom said. "I've done an occasional dumb thing myself."

"Like what?" Megan asked with a grin.

"Well, there was the time that I erased all of the teacher's notes on the board and replaced them with cartoons of Mickey Mouse," he said.

"That was back in sixth grade. It doesn't count," Megan said.

"Well, how about the time I mowed Mrs. Spencer's flower beds instead of her lawn?"

Megan smiled. "That was in seventh grade. Those examples date too far back. Haven't you done anything stupid more recently?"

"Last year I really blew it when I let myself be talked into chairing the Junior Prom Committee."

"How can you say that? You did a fantastic job. Everyone said it was the best prom ever," Megan told him.

Tom waved his hand, dismissing her praise. "Oh, I know I did a good job," he said. "It's just that I spent the whole dance working instead of enjoying the evening with the girl of my dreams."

"I'm sorry," Megan said. "I wish I had known. I would have danced with you."

"Very big of you," Tom teased. "I know," he added suddenly. "You can dance with me now."

"Here?" Megan giggled. "On the beach? In the rain?"

Tom grabbed her hand and spun her under his arm. He pulled her toward him, laid his cheek against hers, pointed their arms forward and led them in a tango down the beach.

"Da dum, dum, dum. Da, da, da, da, da, dum!"

he hummed. "Dip!" he called, as he bent her over backward toward the waves.

Their faces were inches apart. She stared into his blue eyes, transformed now into black pools in the night.

This was the same Tom she had known since grade school. The same Tom who had joined her in countless goofy stunts. But somehow, he was also a different Tom.

In the moonlight sifting through the soft cloud cover, he looked more handsome and mature than he ever had.

She wondered what it would be like to kiss him.

9

Instead of kissing her, however, Tom pulled her upright then threw back his head and laughed.

"What's so funny?" Megan demanded.

"You," he said. "You weren't scared at all."

"Scared of what?"

"Any other girl," Tom said, "would have been afraid I'd drop her in the water."

"That *would* be a typical Tom Hooper thing to do," Megan said calmly.

"Yes, it would," Tom replied, pulling her close again and continuing to tango down the water line.

"And it would be a typical Megan Becker thing to retaliate," she said. "To find some sneaky way to get you back . . ."

"When I least expected it," Tom finished.

"We know each other too well, Tom."

They stopped dancing and stood side by side, staring out at the lights of two ships cruising the horizon. Though the misty, silken blackness enveloped her in safety, Megan couldn't stop thinking about her narrow escape earlier.

"You're still upset about what happened back at Dune Buggies, aren't you?" Tom asked after a few minutes had passed.

Megan nodded. "I wish I didn't always feel compelled to be the class clown."

"To make a fool of yourself for a laugh?" Tom supplied.

"Exactly."

"I feel the same way," he said. "I'd really like to settle down, take life a little more seriously, but people won't let me. They rely on us, Megan, to be their entertainment."

"Being the life of the party has worn a little thin lately," Megan said, shuddering at the thought of Jason's lewd suggestions.

"Don't get me wrong. I still want to have fun. I still want to be crazy sometimes," Tom said.

"Me, too. It's just that lately, I've begun to think more about life after high school."

"Me, too. My parents are gung ho on my going to college, but I'm not sure I *want* to go right into college after high school. For one thing, I don't know what I want to major in. I know too many adults who spent four years in college studying a particular subject and, then got a job having nothing to do with what they studied. It's like when they went to college they were just too young to really know what they wanted."

"Tell me about it," Megan said. "My mom is a data processor, but she always complains about not having a more glamorous career. And my dad is a pilot. Most people think that's a pretty glamorous career, but *he* wishes he had majored in business.

"Sometimes I think that when Sara and I move out of the house, my parents will go back to school to prepare for completely new careers."

"I've been thinking about living on my own," Tom said. "Not because of the good it would do my parents, but because of the good it would do *me*. I don't think I'd act crazy all the time if I *had* to be responsible. My parents would probably be shocked at the change."

"I know mine would," Megan agreed. "Lately, every little thing I do sends them into fits."

Tom let the water lap up on his toes as he stared pensively into the shallows. "Yeah, moving out certainly will be different. Exciting and new and scary."

"That's for sure." Megan laughed. "I'll tell you one change I'm looking forward to. Shannon Dobbler's being out of my sight forever! She's just so vindictive."

Tom turned to look at Megan.

"Shannon thinks nothing of destroying people's reputations for her own personal gain," Megan continued angrily.

"What now? Did something happen after the scene on the beach this morning?"

"You haven't heard?" Megan asked.

"Heard what? I spent the afternoon fishing with my buddies from student council."

"Shannon managed to get Trevor fired. She told her father a bunch of lies about why Trevor banned Mike from the beach and I guess he told his pals at the Cabana Banana. Anyway, not only did Trevor lose his job, but his city lifeguard certificate was suspended for a whole month!"

"That's awful! That's more than awful. It's disgusting!"

"*And* Shannon has put together a team from Leesville, and she's going to use her father's influence to help them win the scavenger hunt."

"She can't do that!"

"How much do you want to bet? Shannon will stoop to *any* level to get what she wants. She's had her revenge on Trevor for kicking Mike off of the beach, and now she's after me, I guess."

"What makes you think that?" Tom wondered.

"Because on the pier earlier she made a point of telling me she was going to win the treasure chest. It's like she's after everyone who won't bow down to her every whim.

"She hates me because I didn't stay at the Flamingo with the rest of the cheerleaders. She hates Alyssa because she broke up with Brock. And I guess she just hates Gabby because she thinks Gabby somehow spirited me away from the cheerleaders."

"And now she hates me," Tom said, "because I sided with Trevor against her."

"Shannon Dobbler has been running Leesville High for too long," Megan declared. "Someone has to show her that we're not afraid of her threats. That's why we've decided to enter the scavenger hunt and beat her at her own game."

"You're going to cheat better than she does?"

"No, silly. With Trevor's help, we're going to make sure she *doesn't* cheat."

Megan turned to Tom and placed her hands on his shoulders. "Tom, I really need you."

Tom stood perfectly still for a long moment. Then he moved his arms ever so slowly and put them around Megan's waist.

His voice was low and husky.

"You don't know how long I've been waiting to hear you say that. Of course I'll be there for you."

"You'll do it?" Megan cried jubilantly. She jumped out of his almost embrace and executed a victory dance on the sand. "Oh, this is great! I wouldn't have asked you if I weren't desperate," she rattled on. "But I really need a partner for the treasure hunt. I've tried and tried to meet my perfect dream guy and team partner all in one, but I've had zero luck in the boy department."

Tom stiffened and then put his hands in his pockets. He drew a circle in the sand with his toe.

Suddenly, Megan realized that Tom wasn't sharing her excitement. "What's wrong?" she asked.

"You've come to the wrong person. I'm not a last resort kind of guy."

"Oh, you mean I should have given you more

notice? Well, I would have, but I just assumed you were already on the student council team. If you are, can't you get off? They could find another guy to take your place . . ."

"I'm not on the student council team," Tom said quietly.

Then, the realization of her mistake hit her all at once. She had hurt his feelings.

"Oh, Tom," Megan said. "I'm sorry. You must feel as if you were my very last choice, but that's not true. I thought of you first; really, I did."

"But you asked me last," Tom said.

"Will you *please* be on our team?" Megan pleaded. "I really do ne— I mean—I think you'd be the best person to complete our crew. You're a fast thinker, very creative, and the most determined person I know."

Megan laid her hand on his arm, but he shrugged it away. "I'll think about it."

"Okay," Megan said slowly. "But you have to let me know soon."

Tom pulled his hands out of his pockets and looked at his watch. "I'd better go," he said abruptly. "I'm late for a date." He bent down to retrieve his shoes.

"A date?" Megan asked, surprised at the

small stab of jealousy she felt right about heart level.

Tom's grin was lopsided and looked sort of forced. "I *do* have a life other than rescuing damsels in distress, you know." He started to jog backward, toward the boardwalk. "See ya!"

"But, Tom," Megan called after him. "What about the team?"

"I'll let you know," he called back.

"He'll do it," Megan said aloud to herself as Tom disappeared into the bright lights in the distance.

"Yes, he'll do it. Tom won't let me down," she said with more confidence than she felt. She started to walk back to the condo, dragging her feet in the sand.

In her mind, she went back over their conversation. What had gone wrong? At first, Tom had said he would be glad to help her. Then, he had seemed offended and only agreed he'd think about it. Had he really been so hurt by her not having asked him to be part of the team earlier?

He must be teasing me, she thought. But she really didn't believe that he was.

The next day, Megan stayed home alone for a while in the morning, waiting for Tom to call or to come over.

When he didn't show, she went out, hoping to find him on the volleyball court or sunbathing on the beach. But Tom Hooper wasn't anywhere to be found.

Megan trudged along the boardwalk. She tried to window shop, but her heart wasn't in it. She looked down the beach and could just make out the colorful sail of Dylan's sailboard, skimming across the top of the waves.

She knew she could join Alyssa and Dylan. He had offered to teach her how to wind surf, but she just didn't feel like being with them.

Gabrielle and Trevor had invited her to ride with them to Isla de los Pájaros Libres, but she had refused, telling herself she didn't want to intrude on their privacy.

And there was really no one else to hang out with. None of her old crowd would have anything to do with her because of the Dobbler curse.

But this morning, she couldn't even get worked up about Shannon. Even the thought of scouting the beach for a "last fling" candidate no longer interested her. The only thing on her mind was finding Tom.

Megan reached the end of the boardwalk and stood looking at the BICYCLES FOR RENT sign. *If I had any money*, she thought, *a long ride might clear my head.*

She sighed and kept on walking. No friends. No money. No goal beyond whipping the pants off of Shannon Dobbler in the scavenger hunt.

She looked down at her arms.

On top of everything else, I'm peeling.

Megan went back to the condo, fixed herself a late breakfast, and lay down in her bed.

"Heard from Tom?" Gabrielle asked when Megan had gotten up from her nap and had joined her friends in the living room. "We can each pitch in an extra dollar to help pay for your share of the entry fee," she added, "but it won't do us any good if Tom doesn't show."

"He'll show," Megan told them again. "You know Tom. He's probably making us sweat as a joke."

Megan's laugh wasn't even convincing to herself. She knew she should have told the others that Tom hadn't really promised to join them. But she had been so sure he would come. For some reason, her mind was made up. It was Tom or no one.

Megan left her friends inside and went out onto the balcony. The day had become somewhat overcast. Megan sat down and pretended to watch the clouds scurry across the sky. In reality, she was hoping to catch a glimpse of Tom strolling toward their condo.

Megan sighed. She knew she had to apologize to Tom for the way she had treated him last night. He was her good friend and she had acted as if his feelings didn't matter. She had actually told him that he was only the stand-in for the "boy of her dreams"!

Hah! The idea of her finding true love before the end of spring break was fading fast. At that moment, finding Mr. Right didn't mean as much to her as finding Tom and saying she was sorry. Even if he had decided not to join their team, which would mean they couldn't participate in the scavenger hunt, she still had to apologize.

"Do you know what Trevor did?" Gabrielle asked as she and Alyssa joined Megan on the balcony. "He contacted a friend of his mother's who's the chairperson of the Merchants Association and told him he'd heard of a plan to cheat. His friend promised that all teams will have to switch lists at the last moment to prevent any foul play."

"Oh, good," Alyssa said. "So even if Shannon *did* get a peek at her list, she'll have to start from scratch just like everyone else."

"No one but us will know the real reason for the switch, and no one but Shannon will care," Gabrielle said. "I can't wait to see the expression on her face when the hunt committee exchanges her list for a new one."

"That will be rich," Megan agreed. "Say, why don't we go over to Dune Buggies a little early? I heard that some of the teams come in costume."

Megan hoped her friends would believe her enthusiasm was real. How could she tell them that she was worried Tom might not show up?

She had never seen him act the way he had last night—so hurt and vulnerable.

"I'm ready," Alyssa said. "Dylan is meeting us at one-thirty."

"Good. The hunt officially starts at three o'clock. Trevor has to work for his uncle this morning, but he said he would meet us by two."

"Is he going to have a permanent job with his uncle?" Megan asked.

"I don't think so," Gabrielle said as she held the door open for her friends. "I think it was just a coincidence that Steve had some extra work at the same time Trevor was out of a job."

The girls headed down the stairs and out onto the beach, walking the now familiar path past the Cabana Banana to the boardwalk, where Dune Buggies stood out from among the wide variety of souvenir shops and eateries.

"What kind of job is Trevor looking for?" Megan asked. "You know, this could turn out to be a good opportunity for him. He might find something he likes a lot better."

"Didn't you say he loves boats and that he's had a lot of experience on them?" Alyssa asked. "Maybe he could hire onto someone's crew."

Gabrielle's smile was uncertain. "Maybe," she said. "I'd like to see him do something with his art, but the decision isn't mine to make. Trevor has to do what's right for him."

"Have you told him yet that you're coming back for the summer?" Alyssa wondered.

"No."

"Why not? Don't you think that would give him something to look forward to?"

Gabrielle stopped for a minute to shake the sand out of her shoes. "I've learned a lot about Trevor in the past few days," she began. "The most important thing I've discovered is that he's very proud. I'm afraid if I told him right now that I was coming back to be with him, he would feel like I was doing it out of obligation or pity."

"Heavy-duty stuff," Megan said.

"For sure," Gabrielle agreed.

"On the other hand," Alyssa said, "it might comfort him to know that you care enough to stand by him whether he has a job or not."

Gabrielle smiled ruefully. "I've thought of that, too."

The girls arrived at Dune Buggies a little after one o'clock, and already teams of people were gathered on the sand in front of the club.

The costumes worn by the pirates in attendance were nothing compared to the zany attire of some of the teams. The group closest to them were wearing trench coats and visored caps, à la Sherlock Holmes. Across the way, six girls in purple wigs, miniskirts, and tube tops huddled together. Another team was dressed as turtles, and another, as a bevy of saloon girls.

"Incredible," Alyssa said.

"I've never seen anything like it," Gabrielle agreed. "I feel a bit underdressed."

"At least we'll be comfortable," Trevor said as he joined the girls.

Megan nodded to Trevor and then continued to scan the growing crowd for Tom. She didn't see him anywhere. She tried to remain positive as more and more people arrived, but her spirits were rapidly sagging.

Her friends were all talking excitedly and pointing over at Shannon's team who had just joined the crowd. How was she going to tell them that Tom wasn't coming after all?

Megan's thoughts were interrupted by the voice of Rick Brick, Dune Buggies' D.J. "Welcome, all you scavengers," he announced from the platform. "Welcome to the tenth annual Billy Bowlegs Scavenger Hunt sponsored by WBCH and the Coconut Beach Merchants Association. Are you having a good time so far?"

A cheer went up from the crowd.

"All right. Then let's get started. On the table in front of me is the official six-hour hourglass filled with genuine Coconut Beach sand."

"Guys," Megan said miserably. "I don't think Tom is coming. I don't think we're going to be able to enter."

"There's still time," Dylan said confidently. "I'm sure everything will work out."

Megan looked at her watch. "With only three minutes to go?" she asked. *Oh, well,* she thought. *At least I know that Shannon won't be able to cheat.* From where she stood, Megan could see Shannon's smirking face and the blustering behavior of Brock and the other guys.

"Look, guys, it's all my fault," Megan said as she turned back to face her friends. "I'm the one who got us into this mess. I'll go and grab some innocent bystander to join our team. And I'll pay everyone back when I get home."

"Don't worry, Megan," Trevor said. "It might be nice to watch from the sidelines anyway. We can come back in six hours for the closing ceremony."

Megan shook her head and started to turn away. Trevor stopped her.

"Listen," he said. "They're making the starting announcements."

"Okay, fellow pirates," Rick said. "I'm going to read out the name of the person on your team's registration form and that person will come up and collect the team's sealed lists. You will pay your entry fee at that time and give us a list of your teammates. Remember, now. No cheating. We'll be counting for six heads as you check out."

Ready to sink into the ground, or to leave before anyone could notice she was missing, Megan didn't hear her name being called.

"Rick called your name, Megan," Gabrielle said, shaking her friend's shoulder. "Go get our packet."

She pressed a wad of money into Megan's hand and gave her a push toward the platform.

What? Megan thought as she made her way to the officials' table. *There must be some mistake. I never even filled out the registration form! In fact, I gave it to Gabrielle!*

When she reached the officials' table, Megan found Tom waiting for her there. "You came!" she cried.

"Of course I came. I couldn't let my best girl down, now could I?"

Megan handed over her team's money, and an official handed her a sealed envelope with the word "PAID" stamped in red across it.

Megan looked up at Tom. Tom just smiled and handed her a daisy. She held it to her nose to smell it and a stream of water hit her in the face.

"Thanks, I deserved that," she admitted as she wiped her face with the back of her hand.

Tom chuckled. "As I said before, you're the only girl I know who doesn't freak out at my little jokes."

Tom started off in the direction of their teammates but Megan put out her hand to stop him.

"Before we join the others, there's something I have to say to you."

Tom turned to face her. He put up his hands in mock horror, as if bracing himself for a trick.

"This isn't a joke, Tom. I'm sorry for the way I acted last night. You must think I'm ten kinds of a jerk."

"I accept your apology," he said seriously. "You didn't know."

"Didn't know what?" Megan asked.

"Never mind," Tom said quickly. "C'mon. We have to get back to the others. It's almost time to start the hunt."

As she followed Tom, Megan heard Rick announce the names for the last few teams. "Wein-geroff, Wilson, and Zabinski," he said. "Come get your envelopes, please. Will everyone please hold on to your unopened envelopes until I give the signal."

When Megan and Tom had rejoined their friends, Rick continued with his announcement. "There has been a surprise change in plans, just to keep things interesting."

"Here it comes," Trevor said.

Rick cleared his throat.

"Everyone take your envelope," he instructed, "lift it high over your head . . ."

Several hundred white envelopes rose in the air.

". . . and exchange it with your neighboring team. Now, no cheating. We'll know if you've exchanged envelopes or not, because each team was given a numbered envelope. We'll compare that number with your new number as you check out of the area today."

There was some general good-natured grumbling as the envelopes were passed. Gabrielle nodded toward Shannon and her team.

"Do you think she suspects we had anything to do with the switch?" Gabrielle asked.

Just then the whistle signaling the time to rip open the envelopes blew. Shannon looked in their direction and stuck out her tongue.

"Very mature," Alyssa commented.

"What would her father say?" Gabrielle quipped.

Trevor laughed. "So, now that we've evened everyone's chances, let's get on with the hunt!"

Tom tore open the envelope and handed the lists to Megan to read aloud.

"It says here," Megan told them, "that we have a choice. There are two lists, one long, and one short. We can collect all of the things on the long list." Megan quickly scanned it. "It's made up of everyday items—a pencil, a roll of toilet paper—that sort of thing. Or, we can work with the bonus list. *It* has only three items."

"We should definitely take the longer list," Gabrielle said. "It should be easier to find a lot of simple items than to find three complicated ones."

Megan disagreed. "I say we take the shorter list. We can split up in pairs and each pair can look for one item. How hard can that be?"

Alyssa put one hand between the two squabblers and with the other, neatly extricated the lists from Megan. "While the two of you are arguing, the rest of the teams are getting a head start. I think we should let Trevor decide. He's the one who knows the area."

Trevor examined both lists and pointed to the short one.

"I told you so," Megan said proudly.

"The items are the brass ring from the carousel in the Salt Air Amusement Park, a life preserver from the *Party Animal* yacht, and a sailor who has both a left shoulder tattoo and a pierced ear. By the way, that's in honor of Billy Bowlegs," Trevor explained.

"What's so hard about catching a brass ring?" Megan asked. "I've grabbed lots of them on the carousel back home."

"Well, there are two difficulties. First of all, the amusement park is twenty miles away," Trevor said.

"And the rules of the contest say you can't use cars," Dylan supplied.

"Bikes?" Alyssa asked.

"Bikes are allowed," Dylan said. "And walking, swimming, or boating. Just no cars."

"Good thing someone read the rules," Megan commented.

"As soon as Tom told Trevor and me that he

was in for sure, we studied the rule book," Dylan explained.

Megan put her hands on her hips and glared at her friends. "You mean you guys knew all along that Tom was coming and you let me worry myself sick?"

Dylan and Trevor just shrugged their shoulders. Alyssa and Gabrielle bent their heads over the long list.

Megan turned to Tom, ready to chastise him, but then thought better of it. There would be plenty of time for a little heart-to-heart talk later.

"Let's break up into teams," Tom suggested quickly. "Megan and I can ride out to the amusement park and go for the brass ring."

Trevor and Gabrielle offered to borrow a life preserver from the *Party Animal*. "I know where Captain Mac usually hangs out," Trevor said. "He's elusive, but I think I can find him."

"That leaves the tattooed sailor with the earring for us," Alyssa said to Dylan.

"Why don't you just go and get a tattoo and pierce your own ear, Dylan?" Megan suggested.

"After you!"

"Don't worry. We'll find our sailor," Alyssa said as she tore the long list into three sections.

"In the meantime, while we're looking for the big stuff, let's pick up as many of the small items as we can along the way. Just in case."

"Sounds like a good plan," Tom said as he took his and Megan's third of the list. "We'll rendezvous back here at eight-thirty, a half an hour before the hunt officially ends."

"Everybody synchronize their watches," Megan said. "I've always wanted to say that!"

Tom put his lips together and mimicked the sound of a cavalry trumpet. "Da, da, da, da, daa!"

"Charge!" Trevor shouted.

As soon as they had checked out with the officials, Megan and Tom raced for the bicycle rental shop, where attendants were loaning the bikes to scavenger hunt contestants.

"No charge today," a freckle-faced teen told them. "It's our donation to the hunt."

"Thanks," Tom said.

"Wow. We got there just in time," Megan remarked a few minutes later as they headed down Oceanview Street. "The shop was almost out of bikes."

"Yeah," Tom said, pedaling up beside her. "I'm not sure we could have made it if we'd had to walk forty miles."

"I'm in good shape, but not *that* good shape."

"Your shape looks pretty good to me," Tom quipped.

"Thanks."

"Except for that scaly stuff on your nose," Tom continued.

"Oh, you!" Megan took a swing at him and missed.

"Pay attention to the road, lady. You almost ran over that grate." Tom took his hands off of the handlebars and used them to make a monster face.

"Yooooou never knoooow what lurks beneath the streeeeets," he moaned.

His bike hit a bump and almost sent him flying.

"Now, who's not paying attention to the road?"

"I meant to do that," Tom said innocently.

"Right."

Megan laughed. She was glad that their misunderstanding hadn't affected their friendship. Still, as they turned the corner from Oceanview Street onto Palm Avenue and headed out of town toward the amusement park, Megan wondered if she should try to talk to Tom again about what had happened on the beach the night before.

Megan still wasn't sure herself what had happened. Or what Tom had meant earlier at Dune Buggies when he had said, "It's okay. You didn't know."

Megan shook her head and concentrated on pedaling at an even, road-devouring speed. She looked over at Tom who was keeping perfect pace with her in the bike lane.

Was he thinking about her?

He turned his head and grinned. "How are you doing, Freckle Face?"

"Better than you, String Bean," she said, calling him by his own fifth-grade moniker.

"Who says?"

"I do!"

"Prove it!"

"Okay, I will!"

They pedaled faster, picking up speed on the flat road. Megan laughed as the wind whistled through her hair. She bent low over the handlebars, striving for the advantage.

It had always been like this between them. Friendly competition. Goofing around together. Telling secrets to each other. That's what friends were for, after all. Then why did she have this funny little feeling down deep? Megan didn't have time to think about it now.

First she had to win their bike race.

An hour later, Megan and Tom sailed into the Salt Air Amusement Park, locked their bikes at the rack, and headed for the carousel.

The park was decorated in the same quaint, seaside style as the older parts of the Coconut Beach; the park's shops could easily have been transplanted from the boardwalk. The rides were painted with details reminiscent of antique county fairs. Flags flew from the tops of jewel-colored tents.

Megan and Tom turned the corner at a big game booth and the carousel loomed in front of them, the centerpiece of the entire amusement park.

"Trevor said there were two problems involved with getting the brass ring. The first problem was the distance to the park," Tom commented thoughtfully, looking up at the elaborate, three-story carousel. "He never did get around to telling us what the second problem is."

"Money for tickets?" Megan suggested as they approached the ticket booth.

"No charge to scavenger hunt contestants," the attendant told them when they explained their reason for being there. "You can ride free if you show me your official list."

Megan produced the folded-up slip of paper, and a moment later, she and Tom took the two biggest horses they could find on the outside row of the first level.

Around and around they went to blaring music from the sixties.

"Where's the brass ring?" Megan asked impatiently when they had circled five or six times.

In front of her, Tom shrugged. "I think it belongs on that clown's extended arm, but so far, I haven't seen it."

"Maybe it's on the next level up?" Megan suggested.

When the carousel stopped, they climbed the stairs to the second level. On this level, the animals were more exotic. Megan chose a camel, and Tom mounted a zebra right behind her. The bell rang and they were off again.

"There's another happy clown," Megan said as they went around. "No ring, though."

Suddenly a child yelled from the bottom level. "I got it! I got the brass ring!"

Megan and Tom looked at each other. They were totally confused.

"But we were just down there," Tom said. "*I* didn't see a ring."

A little girl next to them laughed. "That's what makes this carousel so fun," she said. "You never know when or where the ring will appear. Sometimes it's on the first level, sometimes on the second, or third. You'll be going around and all of a sudden the ring will drop right down into the clown's hand. If you're not right there when it happens, you miss it."

"Great!" Tom said with a roll of his eyes.

Megan giggled. "That must be the *second* difficulty Trevor didn't have the chance to tell us about."

"Hmmm."

The girl pointed helpfully to the clown's arm as they whizzed past. "There's one more problem," she said. "It's too far for most people to reach."

"But a little boy caught it downstairs," Megan reminded her.

"His father probably got it for him," she said simply. "It's so hard because grabbing it wins you a free pass to the park, *and* a ride on all the rides."

"Oh," Megan said dejectedly. "So, what are we going to do?"

"Buy the ring off of that kid?" Tom suggested helpfully.

"With what? I don't have any money."

"And I only have enough for cotton candy," Tom said ruefully.

Megan leaned on the head of her camel. "So, what we have here is a challenge. We have a ring that appears randomly on a three-floor carousel. And, even if we did happen to see it, we probably wouldn't be able to reach it."

"Doesn't sound impossible to me," Tom said. "Besides, I figure we have three more hours before we should head back."

Megan threw back her head and laughed. "Nothing seems impossible when you're around, Tom Hooper."

"I'll take that as a compliment, my dear." Tom reached out and tried to touch the clown's arm and found it was just beyond his fingertips.

"Come here," he said. "Sit in front of me, Meg, my sweet."

"Is this a proposition?" Megan asked.

"A working proposition," Tom said, attempting a wicked grin.

Megan got off her camel and climbed up in

front of Tom on the zebra's saddle, bracing her feet on its forelegs. She leaned back against him and felt the warmth of his chest through his shirt, his breath in her ear.

Suddenly, Megan realized she was having trouble concentrating on the task at hand. She had never felt so . . . so . . . giddy, before.

Tom, seemingly unaffected by their closeness, was still planning. "I figure if we stay on this level the ring will come to us eventually. If I hold on to you and you reach out as far as you can . . ."

"Shut up, Tom!" Megan cried suddenly. "I see it! Hold on to me."

The zebra went down on its pole just as they closed in on the ring. Tom held on to the pole with one hand and to Megan's belt with the other.

Megan ignored the shock of electricity where his hand touched her waist and leaned out toward the ring. "Up, zebra, up!" she ordered. Slowly the crank turned and the zebra inched upward.

"Reach, Megan. You can get it!"

"Almost there!" Megan shouted. "I've . . . I've got it!"

"Hurray!" cried the girl next to them.

"Tell you what," Megan said to her. "If you write down your name and address, we'll mail you the ring as soon as we've presented it to the hunt committee. Then you can get the free pass to the park."

"After all," Tom added, "we never would have gotten it so quickly without your help."

The little girl smiled and reached for the pencil stub Tom held out to her.

"What do you think, Meg? Shall we run away together and join the circus as acrobats?" Tom joked as they exited the carousel.

"Or just run away together!" Megan took off at a run toward the refreshment stand before Tom could see the blush she felt creeping up her neck. *How could I have said something like that? I'm not falling for Tom Hooper. Am I?* Megan thought as she ran.

12

Meanwhile, Gabrielle and Trevor were having a problem. They couldn't find the *Party Animal*.

"I don't understand," Trevor said when they had walked to the pier where it was usually moored and had found the slip was empty. "Captain Mac usually takes his charter folks out earlier in the day. He's always here by now."

"Not today, mate," one of the dockworkers told him. "Today the captain took his boat to Freddy's in Shell Cove for a good swabbing."

"Swabbing?" Gabrielle asked.

"You know, a wash job," the worker said. "Scrape the barnacles off, scrub off the seaweed, oil the prop."

"When is he due back?" Trevor asked.

"He's not," the man said. "Afterward, he's

taking some rich guy and his kin on a Coco Loco evening tour and barbecue at Bird Island."

"Coco Loco?" Gabrielle repeated. This sailor lingo was too confusing.

"Coco Loco is the name of a Travel Agency," Trevor explained.

"If you say so."

"C'mon! We have to hurry, Gabby." Trevor grabbed her hand and pulled her down the dock. "It's a long way to Shell Cove and we want to catch Mac before he heads out to Pájaros Libres."

"Well, what are we waiting for?" Gabrielle dropped his hand and took off at a quick jog down the pier. "Can't we go back into town and get bikes?"

"It would take too long to backtrack," Trevor replied, jogging along beside her.

"Too bad we didn't think to take your boat."

"We may need it yet," Trevor said. "If we miss Mac."

"How far is Freddy's?" Gabrielle asked.

"Five miles," Trevor answered.

"This will give us a chance to talk," Gabrielle said as she matched his stride.

"About what?" Trevor panted. "How long it's been since I jogged any distance?"

"No, about us," Gabrielle said simply. "Is it too soon to talk about us?"

"I've wanted to talk about us ever since that first day on Pájaros Libres. It's strange," he said, "but I feel like I've known you all of my life and I want to know you for the rest of it. I suppose that scares you off?"

"Actually, I feel the same way," Gabrielle said, her arms and legs working in unison with his. "I just thought I was letting the romance of the moment cloud my thinking. What I want most is to have more time to get to know you better, to see if what we have is real, or just some figment of my spring break imagination."

Trevor and Gabrielle picked up their pace, as if their sharing their feelings had given them limitless energy.

"It's not my imagination that you're leaving tomorrow." Trevor kicked a loose pebble in his path. "How are we supposed to find out about what's *real* if we live three hundred miles apart? And please, whatever you do, don't say, 'I promise to write.'"

"How about if I promise to move here after I graduate?"

"That would be better," Trevor said distractedly. Then he stopped and stood completely still.

"What did you say?" he asked through panting breath.

"You're not going to believe this." Gabrielle held her hand to her side and took a gulp of air. "But I've been thinking of moving here ever since Aunt Kate asked me a few days ago to be her roommate for the summer."

"Wait a minute. I seem to remember a conversation at the Blue Moon. You mentioned something about your Aunt Kate needing a roommate for the summer, but I didn't dare hope . . ."

"That first day we met you swept me off of my feet, Trevor." Gabrielle laughed. "I think it was the silly pirate song!"

"I think it was the music of the birds on the island," Trevor said, taking a step toward her.

Gabrielle put her arms around his neck and kissed him, letting the warm spring sunshine wash over her as she listened to the thumping of his heart.

"What happens when summer is over, Gabby?" Trevor asked, when he finally looked into her happy, tear-bright eyes.

"Well, I haven't picked a college yet," she said, pulling playfully on his earlobe. "But I've been considering the suggestions of a trusted friend about art schools in Miami and Saint Augustine . . ."

Her words were muffled against his chest as Trevor enveloped her in a bear hug.

Not far away, Alyssa and Dylan strolled up and down the waterfront in search of a sailor with both a left-shoulder tattoo and an earring. So far they had encountered one old guy with a tattoo, but no earring, and one young fisherman with an earring, but no tattoo.

Between stopping likely prospects, they had managed to pick up several items from the long list. In his backpack, Dylan had a conch shell, a 1978 dime from the Denver mint, and a peacock feather, its colorful eye spot waving above his head.

The two walked out beyond the tourist section and found more piers stretching out into the water. One pier jutted out from a cluster of old-fashioned cottages that had been converted into shops. Alyssa stopped in front of a second-hand store. A sign over the door announced that contestants of the Billy Bowlegs Scavenger Hunt were welcome.

"Maybe we can find some of our items here," she said as she unfolded the list. "How about looking for a tin cup and a wedding veil?"

"We just might find a Red Flyer wagon tongue and a needlepoint picture of a cat here, too." Dylan glanced out toward the end of the pier to where several people were repairing their fishing nets. "When we finish in here, we can check out the people working out on that pier."

"I've just about given up on finding a man with a tattoo and an earring," Alyssa said as they entered into the shop. "I think we should concentrate on finding the rest of the stuff."

"Better safe than sorry," Dylan quipped.

"Hey, look," Alyssa said, pointing excitedly. "There's a wedding veil on that mannequin in the back."

The two made their way through the cluttered aisles to the back of the store where several mannequins were sporting used wedding dresses.

"This is perfect," Alyssa said as she removed

the veil from a mannequin's bald head. "Oh, look." She pointed to a nearby shelf. "There's the tin cup we're after!"

Alyssa put the wedding veil on her head for safekeeping and began rummaging through a bin full of pillows and curtains, hoping to find a needlepoint cat picture. Dylan dug in right beside her.

"Ahem," a voice from behind them said. "What a cozy scene," Brock Jorgensen remarked sourly. "You've barely broken our engagement and now you're ready to jump into marriage with someone else!"

Alyssa turned to face her ex-boyfriend. "You have no idea what you're talking about," she said calmly. "We're collecting items for the scavenger hunt, just like you probably are."

Brock opened his mouth to speak, but Dylan cut him off. "Listen, Brock. You two are bound to run into each other occasionally. Couldn't you at least be civil?"

"I'd like that, Brock," Alyssa said. "Whatever our differences are, we don't have to air them in public."

"How noble of you . . ." Brock began.

He was interrupted by Jenny. She ran down the aisle toward them holding up a silk scarf painted with birds. "Look what I found!" she exclaimed before she saw Alyssa and Dylan behind Brock. "Did you find the bellbottom pants or the—?"

Brock stepped aside and Jenny caught sight of Alyssa. For at least fifteen seconds, no one spoke. It was the longest, most awkward fifteen seconds of Alyssa's life.

Half of her wanted to run and the other half wanted to say the things that she knew needed to be said, right then and there.

Why prolong the inevitable? she thought. *Sooner or later I'm going to have to talk to Brock —really finish it once and for all.*

"Dylan," she said, turning to him and asking for understanding with her eyes. "Why don't I finish up in here while you search the pier for our sailor. I'll meet you outside in about fifteen minutes."

"Are you sure?" he asked.

Alyssa nodded. She watched him as he made his way out of the store.

"Uh . . . I'm going to go search those far racks over there," Jenny said. She waved her hand in the direction of the opposite side of the store. "Uh . . . good luck on the scavenger hunt, Alyssa."

I have to hand it to Jenny, Alyssa thought. *Ninety-nine percent of the time she's obnoxious, but once in a while, she knows how to make herself scarce.*

"We never used to have trouble talking to each other," Brock said after they had stood silently for several seconds.

"I think that's because we never really talked."

"I'm sorry . . ." Brock began.

"Me, too . . ." Alyssa cut in.

"You go first," Brock offered.

"Okay." Alyssa took a deep breath. "I'm sorry for the fight we had on the way down. I'm sorry that I couldn't be the person that you, and everyone else, wanted me to be."

"And I'm sorry for the way I treated you in the Jeep and in front of our friends, both at the café and on the boat. I didn't really mean all of the things I said. I was just so mad at you for walking out on me."

"Your reputation and your friends were always important to you."

"Not as important as you," Brock said quietly.

Alyssa felt a familiar tug at her heartstrings. The same one she had felt every time Brock had apologized with a sweet excuse. But the feeling passed quickly this time and she didn't have the desire to comfort him or kiss their troubles away.

"I know you loved me in your own way, Brock," Alyssa said. "And I'll always have a special place in my heart for you. But it will just never work out. I want to grow and learn and be my own person. I want to make my own decisions."

Brock reached over and fingered the lace on the veil Alyssa had forgotten she was wearing. "When I saw you in this . . . I hoped . . . well, I hoped that maybe we could work things out. I could change, I know I could."

Alyssa smiled sadly and took the veil from her head. "I'm sure you're sincere, but a wedding veil isn't in my future for a long, long time. I don't want you to wait around, hoping I'll change my mind. Because I won't."

"What are you going to do now?" Brock asked, letting his hand drop to his side. "What about your college plans?"

"I'm not sure, exactly. But I've had some ideas since I've been down here. The main thing I want to do is take some time to get to know the new me. I want to go to college someday, but not right away. I think I'll do some traveling first, maybe get a job on a cruise ship and sail around the world."

Brock looked doubtful. She knew he was thinking that she had never done anything on her own in her entire life.

"I have lots of interests that you never knew or cared about," Alyssa added. "Did you know I have an interest in old buildings? I'd like to spend some time *seeing* the famous places I've only read about."

"Couldn't you pursue your *interests* and be married?"

"Maybe I'll get married someday, Brock. When *I'm* ready."

Brock squeezed the bridge of his nose with his fingertips. It was a gesture Alyssa knew well. He made it whenever he was stressed or trying to understand a difficult problem.

"I'm really trying to make sense out of all of this. At first, I was really mad at you for turning my life upside down. But now I realize that your life is topsy-turvy, too. I know one thing, though. Whomever you finally do choose to marry will be one lucky guy."

Alyssa smiled and a tear slipped out of the corner of her eye. "So, I guess this is officially good-bye."

Brock took his hand down from his nose and Alyssa saw that his eyes sparkled with unshed tears.

"I guess so," he said. "It doesn't seem possible. Four great years . . ."

In his voice she heard the echoes of all of the football games, all of the dates, all of their experiences, both good and bad.

"They *were* great years, in many ways," she agreed. "I promise to only remember the good things."

"Me, too."

"Brock!" Jenny called from the front of the store. "We'd better get going."

"Oh, gosh," Alyssa said, glancing at her watch. "I told Dylan I would meet him. I'd better get going, too."

There was a moment of awkward silence. Then Alyssa reached up, hugged Brock, and gave him a kiss on the cheek.

A moment later, she left the store and ran down the pier in search of Dylan.

13

Megan and Tom rode furiously back along the road to town, singing at the top of their lungs.

"I'd ride my bike more at home if Leesville had some of these great bike trails," Tom commented.

"Leesville does have bike trails," Megan argued.

"I meant bike trails with decent scenery. I don't consider a jaunt through the industrial section of town a fun Saturday afternoon outing."

"But think of all the factory workers who save gas by riding their bikes to work. Those workers are very important to the community," Megan said.

"So you have a community conscience now?" Tom teased.

Megan put her feet back on the pedals. "I've always had a community conscience. But, people have a hard time seeing beyond the shell. I'll always be the class clown and 'Becker the Wrecker,' at least to everyone at school."

"That's another reason I'm looking forward to graduation," Tom said. "I want to break out of my image around people who won't continually bring up my past exploits."

"A fresh start," Megan remarked thoughtfully. "I think we both deserve it."

Suddenly, she slammed on her brakes, almost sending herself over the handlebars.

"Stop!" she yelled.

Tom leaped off of his bike and caught it, lifting it off the ground, its wheels still spinning. "What? Flat tire?"

"Nope." Megan grinned. She set her kickstand and walked over to a clump of palm trees next to the road. "Look," she said, pointing up. "A coconut boat."

"When I read that on the list," Tom said, peering up at the long, stiffly folded seedpod, "I thought it was referring to a boat *carved* out of a coconut shell."

Megan giggled. "I've been watching for one

of these ever since we left the amusement park. I saw some farther back, but the trees were too tall."

"*This* tree is pretty tall," Tom said, mentally measuring the long, curved trunk.

He stepped back a few yards and ran toward the tree, leaping as high on the trunk as he could go. For three seconds he looked like an expert, his feet braced on either side of the trunk, his fingers gripping the bark.

Then his feet began to slip. "Spiked shoes would be nice," he said as he slid, inch by inch, down the tree.

"Let me try." Megan spit on her hands. "How hard can it be?"

Tom folded his arms and waited. "Go for it."

"You don't think I can do it? Watch this!"

Megan looped her arms around the tree and straddled it with her legs. She moved her arms up and then used them to pull her body up. Then she hugged the trunk with her knees while she lifted her arms again.

This technique worked until she ran out of energy.

"I got that far in my first leap," Tom teased as she, too, started to slip to the ground.

Tom and Megan stared up at the innocent

little coconut boat nestled in the canopy of fronds.

"Fall!" Megan commanded.

Tom reached down and grabbed a few baby coconuts that had fallen before they were ripe. He pelted the boat with coconut bombs, but it held fast.

"There has to be a way," Megan said. "Give me a boost."

Tom laced his fingers together and Megan put her foot into his hands. She hoisted herself up the trunk, clinging desperately to the smooth bark.

"I can't reach," she said. "I'm only about two feet away, though."

"Try getting on my shoulders," Tom offered. "That should be easy. Just think of me as the top of the cheerleaders' pyramid."

Tom lifted her higher and she stepped gently onto his shoulders. She felt his muscles ripple under her feet as he steadied her ankles.

Slowly Megan rose, keeping her balance against the tree. Finally, when she had found footholds, she pulled away from Tom, grabbed the tip of the coconut boat, and yanked.

"It's stuck."

"Want to use my pocket knife?"

"I can't reach the place where it's hooked on."

"We can't quit now," Tom's voice came from below. "Twist it."

Megan twisted and yanked and twisted some more. "Look out below," she yelled as two coconuts came crashing down.

"Are you trying to kill me?" Tom asked pleasantly.

"Not a chance," Megan said. "I've got it. I'm coming down."

Just as she was bending her knees to lower herself gradually, her foot slipped and she found herself clinging to the palm trunk with no support.

"Help?" she squeaked.

"Jump," Tom instructed. "I'll catch you."

"Why me?" Megan wailed. She let go of the trunk and pushed herself out from the tree. Tom grabbed her around the waist as she dropped. He stumbled backward but was able to keep the two of them on their feet.

Megan turned to thank him, expecting Tom to release her, but he didn't. They were very close, their noses almost touching. Megan thought of the moment on the beach the other night when she was sure Tom was going to kiss her, and the same electric feeling of anticipation did a dance on her nerve endings.

"Tom?"

"Megan?"

A loud horn blew. The spell was broken and Tom released her.

"It came from down there," Megan said. She waved her hand in the direction of a group of rental cottages and a small dock.

"Does that say what I think it says?" Tom asked.

"The *Party Animal*," Megan squealed. "I can't believe it. Trevor and Gabby are probably looking all over town for this yacht, and it's hiding out over here!"

"Maybe they already got the life preserver," Tom said.

"Or maybe not. What if they got to the pier after the *Party Animal* had left?"

"Well, why don't we at least *ask* the captain if Trevor and Gabby have borrowed the life preserver yet."

Leaving their bikes on the side of the road, Megan and Tom clambered down a set of wooden steps to the dock where the captain of the yacht was greeting passengers. Two crew members were just putting up a banner which said, *"Bird Island Barbecue, Compliments of Coco Loco Tours,"* above the boarding ramp.

Just before they reached the dock, Megan stopped and stared hard at a familiar blond-haired figure slipping through a door on the center deck.

"Shannon is on the *Party Animal,"* she whispered to Tom. "Do you suppose her team has to find a life preserver, too?"

"Could be that a lot of teams have to bring back life preservers," Tom speculated.

"That does it," Megan declared. "No way am I going to let Shannon float away with *our* life preserver! C'mon!"

They followed the last group of passengers up the boarding ramp and greeted the captain, who now stood at the top.

"Are you Captain Mac?" Megan held out her hand to shake his.

"That I am," he said. "Are you two kids part of the Coco Loco trip to Isla de los Pájaros Libres?"

"No, we're friends of Trevor Jamison. We were wondering if he had caught up with you today," Tom explained. "We're participating in the Billy Bowlegs Scavenger Hunt, and Trevor was in charge of borrowing a life preserver from the *Party Animal.*"

"I haven't seen Trevor today," the captain said. "But my ship has been down at Freddy's for an overhaul and now I'm taking this charter trip to the island. He probably couldn't find me."

"Would you mind if we borrowed an extra life preserver?" Megan asked. "We'll bring it back first thing tomorrow morning."

"No problem at all," Captain Mac said. "There's a whole bunch of extras in the linen closet, next to the galley on the main deck."

"Thanks," Tom said as soon as they had obtained directions.

"Make it quick," Captain Mac said. "We're leaving in five minutes."

"Don't worry about us," Tom said. "We'll get the preserver and be off in a flash."

"Good luck with the hunt," the captain called. "Remember, I'm counting on you to do your business and be off this ship before she sails."

"No problem!" Megan and Tom answered. Then they took off down the side walkway to the galley and staff area to search for the door marked "Linens."

"Here it is!" Megan cried after a few minutes' search. She turned the knob and opened the door to a small room filled with towels, table-cloths, dust rags, cleaning supplies, and life preservers. "A whole stack of them, just like Captain Mac said."

"Here," Tom said. "I'll lift these brooms and mops out of the way and you grab the preserver on the top of the stack. With the brass ring and now this life preserver, we've got it made."

"Yep," Megan agreed. "This is our lucky day!"

Suddenly, the light went off and the door slammed shut behind them.

"The wind?" Megan whispered.

They heard the sound of Shannon's high-pitched cackle from outside the door.

"The wind doesn't laugh like that," Tom said, fumbling for the light switch. "Great! I just remembered. The switch is outside the door."

Shannon laughed again.

"Let us out, Shannon," Megan shouted. "There are plenty of preservers in here for both our teams."

"Oh, I don't need one of those," Shannon called out. "I stole one from the lounge."

"Why didn't you just borrow it?" Tom asked.

"Because that wouldn't have been as much fun," Shannon snapped. "But you two are going to have *lots* of fun," she added. "Hope you like close quarters because you're going to be in there all night!"

"The captain will let us out," Megan threatened. "And then you'll be in big trouble."

"I'll be long gone by then," Shannon boasted. "In five minutes this yacht will dock at the Coconut Beach pier and my team will win, hands down."

Megan felt the yacht vibrate and begin to chug out into open water. "Five minutes?" she said, forcing a short laugh. "Don't you know this yacht is sailing for Pájaros Libres? You're just as stuck as we are."

14

Alyssa looked up and down the pier, but Dylan was nowhere to be seen.

Could he have been upset at my wanting to speak to Brock alone? she thought worriedly. Brock would have thrown a fit if she had wanted to speak to another boy alone while they were going together.

No, Dylan's not like that. She had to stop comparing Dylan to Brock. They were totally different people.

Just then, Gabrielle and Trevor jogged up to her. "How are you guys doing?" Gabrielle asked. "We're on our way out to Freddy's to track down the *Party Animal*. Want to come?"

"I have to find Dylan first. He's around here somewhere. Let's cross our fingers that he's found a grizzled old sailor with a tattoo *and* an earring. Do these guys actually exist?" Alyssa laughed. "We've been all over town and haven't found one person who fits the bill."

"Sounds as if you're having about as much luck as we are," Trevor said. "We went to the right dock, but we found out that Captain Mac took the yacht to Freddy's to have it overhauled. From there he's conducting a charter tour to Pájaros Libres early this evening."

"What are you waiting for, then?" Alyssa said.

"We were on our way when we saw you standing here," Gabrielle said. "Hey, are you okay? You look a little drained."

"I just had my *final* talk with Brock," Alyssa told her. "It was pretty hard, but I think things will improve now."

"Between you and Brock?" Gabrielle asked.

"No, between me and myself!"

"Hey, everyone," Dylan shouted from the other end of the pier. "Come see who I found!"

The three friends hurried down the pier to join him.

"I found the sailor we've been looking for," Dylan announced with a grin. He pointed to the nearest boat where a young woman in jeans and a tank top was securing her lines.

"Sally," he called, "I'd like you to meet my friends, Alyssa, Trevor, and Gabrielle."

Sally turned around and the tattoo of an eagle in flight was clearly visible on her left shoulder. Gold hoops with tiny fish charms dangled from her ears.

"I'm very pleased to meet you," Sally said as she came toward them and shook hands with all of them. "I have a little more work to do here. The boat sprung a leak while I was out today. But I'll meet you at Dune Buggies at eight-thirty, right, Dylan?"

"Eight-thirty it is," Dylan said. "And, thanks, Sally."

"It's all for a good cause." Sally reached up and touched her ear. "You don't think the judges will care that I have *two* earrings instead of one, do you?"

Trevor laughed. "The list only said to bring in a sailor with a left-shoulder tattoo and an earring."

"I'll remove one for good measure," Sally joked.

"I hope Megan and Tom are having better luck getting the brass ring than we're having finding the *Party Animal*," Trevor said. "We'd better get going if we're going to catch her before she heads out to sea."

"Well, I hate to say it," Sally said, "but on my way in just now, I passed the *Party Animal* chugging along with a load of passengers. They were heading out toward . . ."

"Isla de los Pájaros Libres!" Trevor sighed. He consulted his watch. "Six o'clock. I should have known. They're probably halfway there by now if they expect to barbecue and feed everyone before dark."

"Can we still catch them?" Gabrielle asked. "I'd hate to have come this close and then to lose out."

"If you want, I'll run you over to the Coconut Beach pier as soon as I patch the boat," Sally offered.

"No time to waste," Dylan said. "It's not that far back to town and Trevor's boat if we run."

"Why do I feel as if I've been running all day?" Gabrielle moaned as they all began to jog back through the residential area and to the pier where Trevor's boat was moored.

"Because you *have* been running all day," Trevor answered playfully.

Megan's eyes had become adjusted to the dim light in the closet. She and Tom were sitting on the floor, knees touching. She could just see his outline, leaning against the door.

"Do catastrophes follow you, or has everything that's happened really just been an accident?" Tom asked.

"I'm beginning to wonder," Megan said. "Since I've been in Coconut Beach, it's been one disaster after another. First, Gabby's car broke down and we were picked up by Jason and Chad."

"And we both know what swell guys they are," Tom commented.

"Then I ran out of money and got a terrible sunburn trying to look beautiful for the bikini contest."

"And then T. J. the lifeguard, your prize date for the evening, turned out to be Gabby's boyfriend."

"Then the shark scare and Trevor getting fired."

"And now this."

Megan and Tom were silent for a moment, listening for the sound of footsteps. They both knew the likelihood of someone wandering by was slim. The Coco Loco tour group, and probably the captain, were up on the front deck, dancing to the thumping beat of a calypso band.

"Someone is *bound* to come by," Megan said in an attempt at sounding cheerful.

"Before next week, I hope," Tom said. "I'm getting hungry."

"I think I saw some mints before Shannon turned the lights out." Megan eased herself off of the floor and felt around on the shelves around them. "You know, they were the kind they put under your pillow at night in fancy hotels."

"Anything would do at the moment. I'm thirsty, too."

"Well, there's a sink in here, too." Megan laughed. "We have all the comforts of home!"

"*You're* very observant," Tom remarked. "*I* didn't notice a sink when we came in."

"Ouch! Not that observant. I just bumped my shin on something. I think the sink is in the back corner, behind the, whoops . . ."

Crash!

"Behind the metal water pitchers," she said feebly.

Tom stood up, knocked his forehead against something, tripped over a rolling pitcher, and fell into Megan. They both went down with a thud.

"Mint?" she said from beneath the tangle of

arms, legs, and cleaning supplies. Megan felt around for Tom's mouth and shoved the chocolate covered candy between his lips.

"Mmm, thanks."

"I'd hold off on the water," Megan suggested, popping a mint into her own mouth. "I'm liable to pour it all over your head."

"Listen," Tom whispered as he clutched her hand. "I think I hear someone coming."

Megan couldn't concentrate on listening for footfalls. Her heart was beating a mile a minute. Sitting in the dark, with Tom's hand on hers, was doing strange things to her insides. She felt hot and cold at the same time. Her palms were sweating, but wherever Tom's body came into contact with hers on the floor of that closet, she felt a deliciously icy shiver.

"There it is again," Tom whispered. He untangled himself and crawled to the door.

Tom banged on it and shouted, "Hey out there! Can anybody hear me? We're locked in here!"

"Help!" Megan cried. She crawled up beside him and pounded on the door.

A second later the light went on and a crew member unlocked the door.

"Someone locked us in," Megan told him as

she scrambled to her feet. "We'll clean up the mess. I promise."

The crewman walked away, shaking his head and muttering something about practical jokers and dangerous stunts. Tom held the door open and kept watch for Shannon while Megan quickly restacked the pitchers and replaced the box of mints. Then she took a dime out of her pocket and put it in the box with the empty wrappers.

"Let's get out of here," Tom said when she had done.

"Do you think Shannon's still around?" Megan asked.

"Probably not. Knowing Shannon, she probably threatened to tell her daddy if Captain Mac didn't let her off the boat."

"Now we'll be stuck on this boat until way after the hunt is over." Tom frowned and leaned on the rail.

"I think we'd better find the captain and tell him what happened," Megan said.

They hadn't taken two steps when Megan felt the life preserver she'd taken with her yanked out of her hand. She whirled around and faced Shannon.

"You'll do no such thing!" Shannon sneered.

"You won't say a word to the captain about what happened. If you do, you'll be sorry!"

"What are you going to do, Shannon? Have us walk the plank?" Megan snorted.

Shannon jabbed a finger in front of Megan's face. "You've given me nothing but trouble since spring break started. As of now, you're officially off the cheerleading squad!"

"Sorry, Shannon," Tom interrupted. "You can't do that. Once a person has passed the try-outs, she stays on the squad for a whole year, as long as she keeps her grades up."

"And the last time I checked, my grades were in fine shape," Megan said calmly. "That's more than I can say for your attitude, Shannon Dobbler. You are the most conceited, self-centered person I have ever known. I'm surprised it took me so long to realize it. I guess I wanted so badly to be popular, I put up with all of your crud. But no more!"

"That's right." Shannon smirked. "You have your new little pals to keep you company. I hope you like them a *lot*," she said. "Because once we get back to Leesville, no one else will ever speak to you again."

Tom grinned. "Don't worry, Megan. *I'll* speak to you."

"Stay out of this, Tom!" Shannon shouted. "Or I'll put the deep freeze on your reputation, too."

With a swift move, Shannon pushed Megan up against the rail.

Tom took a step toward her, but Megan shook her head. "No, Tom, this is my fight."

"Yeah, c'mon and hit me," Shannon taunted, sticking out her chin. "I can't wait until everyone hears how you abused me."

"Ha! You're the one who abuses people—Gabby, Alyssa, Trevor—" Megan replied. "Anyone who doesn't do what little Shannon wants."

"If I come home with a black eye, who do you think my daddy will believe? His daughter, or *you*? He'll sue your parents for everything they're worth and then some."

Megan clinched her hands at her sides. "Give me back that life preserver!" she demanded as she grabbed the white ring and gave it a tug.

Shannon tugged back. "Make me!"

Megan pulled with all her might.

At that very instant, Shannon let go. Then, in one quick movement, she reached down, grabbed Megan's ankles and flipped her over the rail.

Megan landed in one of the *Party Animal*'s inflated lifeboats. The fall knocked the wind out

143

of her and as she bumped her head on an oar, the life preserver flew out of her hand and into the water. It was quickly left behind as the yacht sailed on.

"Oh, my head," she moaned as she tried to sit up.

In a flash, Tom jumped into the boat beside her and began to feel her head for lumps. "Are you okay?" he asked as he brushed a stray hair out of her face.

"Isn't that sweet!" Shannon called from above them. "So long, suckers!"

Before Tom could react, Shannon released the locking mechanism on the lifeboat.

Megan grabbed on to Tom's waist. Tom grabbed the oarlocks.

Two seconds later, they landed in the water. In two more seconds, they were soaked by the splash their landing created.

"I will absolutely never forgive that girl!" Megan cried as she watched Shannon and the *Party Animal* moving serenely off into the twilight.

15

"Help!" Megan yelled as loud as she could.

"Forget it," Tom said. "Who would hear you over the sound of the engines and the band?"

Megan collapsed back against the raft's inflated side.

"How's your head?" Tom asked.

"Fine."

"You're sure?"

"Positive."

"What's wrong, then?"

"Are you kidding?" Megan shouted. "We're in a raft in the middle of the Atlantic Ocean. No food. No water. It's getting dark. And we're going to lose the contest, all because of stupid Shannon Dobbler!"

"So, you're having hysterics?" Tom asked mildly.

Megan screamed, long and loud.

"I'm better now," she said finally.

Tom laughed. "I like your style, Megan Becker."

"Thank you."

Tom untied and lifted a piece of canvas at the end of the raft. "Hmm, let's see what's in here."

Tom pulled out a waterproof box. "Ah-ha! First-aid kit, flares, a pair of collapsible oars, and . . . ta da!"

Tom reached farther into the opening and lifted out a life preserver with the words *Party Animal* stenciled clearly on each side.

"Maybe we *are* lucky," she said thoughtfully. "Shannon hasn't won yet. She's heading off in the wrong direction and *we* have the life preserver. All we have to do is row back to Coconut Beach and find the rest of the gang!"

Tom handed her an oar and showed her how to push the buttons to release the expandable sections inside. Then he hooked his oar neatly into the oarlock.

But Megan's oarlock wouldn't twist around in the right direction. She balanced the oar on the side of the boat and took hold of the lock with both hands.

With a mighty yank she turned the oarlock, and as she did, the oar slipped off the side of the raft. She tried to grab it, but a swell took it just out of reach.

"Oh, no!"

"Paddle," Tom commanded.

They each leaned over the sides of the raft and paddled for all they were worth, but the undulating evening sea worked against them.

"I'm sorry," Megan said as she watched the oar slip farther and farther away from the bobbing raft.

Tom took off his shirt.

"What are you doing?"

"I'm going to swim for it. What does it look like?" Tom said.

"Can't we just paddle with one oar, a little on one side and a little on the other?"

"It won't work. We'll just go around in circles."

"But, Tom," Megan said, looking over the rim of the raft into the water. Seaweed waved beneath the surface and even in the deepening twilight, she could make out the shapes of small fish and rocks.

"You don't know what's lurking down there.

147

There might be a stingray, or a barracuda, or a school of jellyfish," she protested.

"Or the Coconut Beach monster," Tom cracked.

Tom slipped easily over the side of the raft, shivering a little as the water came up around his waist, his chest, and then his neck.

Suddenly, Megan stiffened. "How good a swimmer do you think Mike Bibbitt is?" she asked, her eyes on a strange shape she saw moving toward them in the water.

"I mean," she continued nervously, "he wouldn't swim all the way out here just to scare us to death, would he?"

"Of course not," Tom answered as he tread water.

The shape moved closer, a dark shadow cruising just beneath the surface of the water.

"Tom!" Megan said urgently. "Get back in the boat. I think I see a shark!"

"You're kidding, right?" Tom asked.

Megan reached out and grabbed Tom's arm. "I've never been more serious in my life!" she whispered. "Hurry, Tom."

Tom quickly flopped over the side and into the raft, just as a huge hammerhead shark passed beneath the boat.

Megan and Tom yelped with fright and scrambled into the middle of the raft.

"Tom, I'm scared," Megan whispered as she clung to him.

"You're not the only one," he said, his voice shaking.

"I don't see him," Megan said. "Do you think he might have gone away?"

"I doubt it. We're probably too interesting."

Megan hugged Tom tighter. "I don't want to die out here!"

"We're not going to die," Tom told her. "I don't think hammerhead sharks are dangerous."

"How do you know?" Megan asked, her voice still hushed.

"I *don't* know for sure," Tom admitted. "I sure wish I had paid more attention to that Jacques Cousteau special on sharks. All I remember was a woman scientist putting on a suit of chain mail and waving a piece of meat around, hoping a shark would bite her arm."

"That's terrible," Megan said. "I would *never* be brave enough to do that."

Tom was thoughtful for a moment. "I do remember Trevor saying that most shark attacks occurring in Florida happen in the surf, when swimmers are flailing around and acting like a school of mullet. The spinner and black tip sharks strike, and then immediately release when they realize they made a mistake."

"That's very comforting," Megan remarked. "So, we'll only get bitten, not devoured."

"Something like that."

Fifteen minutes went by and there was no further sign of the shark. Megan and Tom began to relax a little.

And then Megan began to be aware of sensations other than those produced by her soggy clothes. She heard her rapidly beating heart. She felt the texture of Tom's skin under her cheek. He was warm despite the cooling night air and she could still smell his cologne. It was kind of minty and it tickled her nose. Without thinking about what she was doing, she rubbed her cheek against his chest and tightened her arms around him.

"I always hoped for this," Tom murmured. "The girl of my dreams wrapped in my arms, alone with me in a romantic setting. Somehow, though, I didn't quite picture it happening *this* way."

Megan was afraid to move. The strange feelings she'd had about Tom in the past few days came rushing upon her now.

She raised her head and studied his face. "Are you kidding again?" she asked quietly.

"I've never been more serious in my life," he confessed.

Megan smiled, and Tom took her hand and laced his fingers through hers.

"I've always been crazy about you," he said. "Ever since fifth grade when we did that funny dance for the talent show."

"It wasn't supposed to be funny."

Tom grinned. "But it was. Admit it."

Megan rolled her eyes and matched his grin. "You're right. It *was* funny. But I worked so hard on planning just the right steps."

"And then you picked someone with two left feet to be your partner," Tom said. "I'm a much better dancer now."

"I know." Megan remembered their tango on the beach.

Why hadn't he told her that night how much he liked her? Then she remembered his response when she'd told him she needed him. Maybe he *had* been trying to tell her, but she had been too busy worrying about her own problems to listen.

Megan sat up and braced herself on the side of the raft.

"If you've always liked me so much," she asked, "why haven't you ever asked me out?"

"The fact that you're always surrounded by at least fifty-seven admirers has had something to do with it."

"I am not! No, really, Tom. Why did you wait so long to tell me?"

"I was afraid you would turn me down," he said simply.

"But you've always treated me like one of the guys. I never dreamed—I mean, I might have made a play for you a long time ago if you had given me the slightest indication . . ."

"I figured it was better to be your friend than one of your rejected suitors," Tom said. "You've dumped a lot of guys along the way."

"Maybe I was waiting for the *right* guy to come along," Megan said softly. "But the *right* guy was never serious for two seconds, so I had no idea he really *was* the right guy. Tom, you're always joking around."

"So are you."

Before she could respond, Tom put his hands on either side of her face and looked deeply into her eyes.

"This isn't a joke," he said.

And then he was kissing her. Megan lost herself in the pure joy of the moment. It seemed as if she had been waiting forever for Tom's kiss. Memories of the wonderful times they had spent together since grade school flashed through her mind as he continued to kiss her. Finally, they leaned back against the raft's padded side, unable to part.

Suddenly, Megan giggled.

"What's so funny?" he asked warily.

Megan shook her head. "Don't worry. It just struck me as funny that my big plan for this spring break was to meet the perfect guy and fall in love."

"And . . ." Tom prompted.

"And I traveled hundreds of miles to fall in love with the boy next door."

Tom grinned. "It *is* convenient for continuing the relationship, however."

"Very true. Uh, Tom?"

"Yes?"

"Shut up and kiss me."

"Happy to oblige," he said. "Anytime at all." And then Tom swooped in for a devastatingly passionate kiss.

Though Megan surrendered herself to his

kiss, she was totally aware of the irony of the moment. They were in an absolutely disastrous situation, stalked by a shark and drifting off to who knew where. Shannon and her team would win the scavenger hunt and their friends would never know what had happened to them. She and Tom would never be seen again.

It was probably the happiest moment of her life.

16

The loud blast of a boat horn shattered their romantic interlude.

Megan and Tom waved and yelled at the small craft coming toward them in the water, almost tipping the raft over in their efforts.

"Over here!" Megan shouted. "We're saved!"

"Too bad," Tom said as he peered through the dusk at the approaching boat. "I was beginning to like it out here."

Megan socked him in the arm.

"Is that Megan?" Gabrielle cried. "And Tom?"

"What are they doing out here?" Dylan asked. "This is nowhere *near* the amusement park!"

Trevor pulled up alongside the raft and cut

the motor. "All aboard!" he called in his best sea captain's voice.

"What are you guys doing here?" Megan asked. "I can't believe it. We're rescued by our own friends!"

"We could leave you out here to be rescued by someone else if you'd like," Trevor teased.

"You know what I mean!" Megan replied. "Get us out of here!"

After Megan and Tom had joined the group in Trevor's boat, the six teammates assessed the situation.

"It's eight o'clock," Dylan said. "Only one hour before the hunt is officially over. We'd better get moving if we expect to get to Pájaros Libres for that life preserver and back to Dune Buggies in time."

Megan reached back into the raft and pulled up the life preserver she and Tom had found there. "No problem. We already have it."

"But Captain Mac needs his lifeboat," Trevor said. "I think we have enough time to run it out to him before we head back to Coconut Beach."

On the way to the island, Megan and Tom took turns telling the others about their encounter with Shannon and their adventures on the yacht.

"I can't believe she locked you in the linen closet," Alyssa exclaimed.

"And pushed you overboard!" Gabrielle cried.

"You could have her arrested for assault," Dylan said.

Trevor shook his head. "We're just glad that you're safe. But that girl needs some serious psychiatric help!"

"I wonder if she figured out a way to get back to the mainland with her precious life preserver? She was really determined to beat us," Tom said. "She probably would have been thrilled if that shark had eaten us."

"Shark!" Alyssa shrieked. "You saw a *shark*!"

Megan and Tom took turns relating the story of the shark.

"If we had died," Megan said melodramatically, "it would have been all Shannon's fault."

"No prize is worth endangering people's lives," Gabrielle said. "I feel sorry for Shannon. She has every material thing that she could ever want. But she doesn't have any true friends."

"I'd rather be me than her, any day," Megan said. She took Tom's hand in the semi-darkness.

No one saw the secret look that passed between them. "Friends are more important than anything."

"Watch for the reef," Trevor instructed Gabrielle, who was sitting in the bow of the aluminum boat. "Use the light under the seat. I know we're close."

Gabrielle shined the light up ahead into the shallow water. "It's to the left," she called. Trevor turned in time and headed around the island to the back side.

"Thanks," he called back. "We make a good team."

As soon as they rounded the southern tip of the island, the *Party Animal* came into view. A big bonfire lit up the picnic area and the aroma of barbecued steaks wafted to them on the breeze.

Tom sniffed the air. "We've come to the right place. Forget the scavenger hunt. Let's eat!"

"There'll be plenty of food at Dune Buggies. The entry fee included a meal, remember?" Megan said.

Tom stuck out his lip and whimpered. "But I'm hungry now."

"You're tough. You can take it," Megan said

with a laugh. "Besides, you had a mint in the closet."

"Oh, right. How could I forget that?" Tom patted his stomach. "I'm so stuffed."

"Shh! Listen," Alyssa said. "I think I hear Shannon!"

Sure enough, Shannon's voice rose loud and clear above the put-put of the boat's motor.

"I tell you, I *have* to get back to Coconut Beach this instant!" she yelled. "I demand that you have one of your crew members ferry me back."

A moment later the friends saw Shannon and Captain Mac standing on the dock.

"My crew members are needed here," Captain Mac's deep, patient voice answered her.

"Your crew members won't have a job after my *father* gets through with them! He can ruin your business! He can have you fired! He can—"

"Now hold it right there, Miss Dobbler," Captain Mac replied. "My business and my boat are privately owned. You can call whomever you like, but it won't do you any good. I'm *not* taking you back to Coconut Beach until this party is over."

"But—"

"And when we do return," he cut her off, "I'll call your father personally and tell him how much he owes me for your passage and for the loss of my lifeboat."

Shannon folded her arms across her chest and turned her back on him. "You'll be sorry!" she threatened.

"Sound familiar?" Alyssa asked.

"Very," Trevor replied in disgust.

"Oh, look, look!" Shannon squealed. "Here comes a little motorboat. I'm saved!" She turned to Captain Mac and smiled at him sweetly. "Oh, please, Captain, sir," she drawled, "couldn't we ask them to take me back to shore?"

"She mustn't be able to see who we are," Megan whispered.

Trevor idled the motor and steered toward the dock. Expertly he switched into reverse and brought the boat to a stop right next to the mooring cleats. He tied the boat on with an expert double half hitch.

"At this point," they heard Captain Mac say, "I would do just about anything to get rid of you, Miss Dobbler."

Shannon turned around to face the crew of the motorboat, a smile plastered across her face.

But the smile disappeared as soon as she saw Megan and her friends.

"Hey, Captain!" Trevor called. "We brought back your lifeboat."

"Great!" he said. "Where did you find it?"

"A couple of miles from here, trying to float out into the shipping channel."

"We're sorry, but we lost an oar," Tom said. "If you'll let us know how much it costs, we'll be happy to replace it."

Captain Mac looked at Tom and then back at Shannon, who was looking at the moon and humming.

"You told me the lifeboat disengaged accidentally," he growled. "But you didn't happen to mention that anyone was on board."

"Oh," Shannon cried innocently. "Did I forget to mention that?"

Captain Mac turned his attention back to the passengers in the boat and Shannon scowled at his back.

"Are you all right? I would never have cast off from Coco Loco if I had known you were still on board."

"There was a little matter of our being locked in a closet," Tom explained.

"And then their being *shoved* overboard and left to drift," Trevor added.

"But we're none the worse for wear," Megan assured him. "The encounter with the shark did take about ten years off our lives, but we'll be fine."

Trevor untied the raft and handed Captain Mac the line. "We'd like to take Ms. Dobbler off your hands," he said politely, "but, as you can see, my boat is full."

Captain Mac nodded seriously, ignoring the obviously empty seat.

Trevor yanked the motor's starter cord and the engine roared to life.

"You can't do this to me!" Shannon shouted. "You can't leave me here stranded!"

"Gee, that's too bad, Shannon," Megan replied. "You should have thought about all the possibilities before you stowed away."

"Yeah, you didn't think anything was wrong with leaving *us* stranded!" Tom remarked. "You'll be lucky if we don't report you to the authorities."

Shannon stomped her foot and her face became a mask of fury. "I'll . . . I'll . . . I'll . . ." she stammered.

"*What* are you going to do, Shannon?"

Gabrielle taunted. "Have Trevor fired? You've already done that!"

"You're not working at the Cabana Banana anymore?" Captain Mac asked Trevor.

Trevor shook his head. "No. And it doesn't look like I'll be lifeguarding anywhere for a while, thanks to Miss Dobbler, here. She told a bunch of lies and managed to get my certificate suspended."

"I'm not going to stand here and listen to this!" Shannon stomped off a few feet and stopped.

"Come to work for me, Trevor," Captain Mac said heartily. "I sure could use a good first mate. And you could hang some of those paintings of yours on the wall of the lounge. They'd spiff the place up a bit, and I think some of my customers would be happy to buy them."

Trevor grinned and reached up to shake Captain Mac's hand. "You've got yourself a deal," he said.

Shannon sidled back toward the boat and made one last attempt to gain a ride back to Coconut Beach. "See, Trevor," she said, "if it hadn't been for my getting you fired, you never would have gotten this fabulous new job. It seems to me that you *owe* me one."

"You are truly incredible, Shannon," Trevor said.

"I know."

Trevor looked at her pityingly. "That wasn't a compliment."

Shannon's mouth opened, but no words came out.

"I'll call you tomorrow, Captain. And, thanks!"

Trevor steered the boat out of the dock, following the channel carefully to avoid the rocks. Just before they were out of earshot, they heard Shannon's whine.

"No! I refuse! I've never done dishes in my life!"

17

Laughter rang out over the water as Trevor gunned the motor and they sped off toward Coconut Beach.

"Hold on!" Trevor shouted above the noise of the wind. "We're going to make it just in time."

Just as she had earlier, when she and Tom were riding their bikes, Megan reveled in the rush of air against her face. She was still pretty wet, but even that didn't matter. Tom was beside her and they were going to make it back to Coconut Beach in time to present their collected items.

The water seemed beautiful now that she had a solid aluminum floor beneath her feet and she could see the lights of Coconut Beach reflecting off the waves in front of them.

With practiced ease, Trevor zoomed his boat

into the dock. Everyone jumped out, and Trevor secured the boat.

"Do you have the brass ring?" Megan asked Tom.

Tom patted his pants pocket. "Right here."

"I've got the life preserver," Megan said, tucking it under her arm.

"And Sally should be waiting at Dune Buggies," Dylan said as he consulted his watch. "Only five minutes left until the deadline! Let's go!"

The six friends ran down the pier and across the sand. Megan and Tom's wet feet made squashing sounds and their shoes collected about a pound of sand, but they pressed on.

Megan could see Rick up on the stage, getting ready to strike the gong which would signal the end of the hunt.

"Wait!" she cried as they lunged through the crowd.

Rick's arm paused midswing. "One final entry into the drawing," he announced. The group piled their goods on a table and presented Sally to the judges.

"Bong! Bong!"

The judge placed a piece of paper with their team's name on it in the big jar next to the treasure chest. It fluttered down to rest on top of all of the other pieces of paper on which were written the names of all the other teams which had also completed their quests.

"We'll choose the name of the winning team after dinner," Rick announced. "Right now, let's chow down!"

The band struck up a rock 'n' roll favorite and the group uttered a collective sigh.

"It doesn't matter whether we win the drawing or not," Megan said brightly. "As far as I'm concerned, we've already won."

"We beat Shannon without cheating or doing anything illegal," Alyssa said.

"And Trevor has a new job," Gabrielle said happily.

Megan grinned and took Tom's hand. "And," she said, "all three of us girls have found the boy of our dreams!"

There was a moment of stunned silence.

"You and Tom?" Gabrielle finally managed to ask. "I mean, I knew the two of you were meant for each other . . ."

"So did I," Alyssa said. "But how did you—?"

Megan didn't have a chance to answer. Tom had grabbed her and they were locked in a kiss that looked pretty serious.

Trevor looked at Dylan. "I think he has the right idea," he said.

"You'll get no argument from me," Dylan replied.

A moment later, all three girls were pleasantly occupied.

"This has been the longest and the shortest week of my life," Gabrielle said as they were loading her Mustang the next day for the trip home.

"I'll never forget it," Megan said. "And Tom will be right there to remind me. Hey! Thanks for helping us find each other."

"What do you mean?" Alyssa asked.

"Didn't you think I'd figure out that you guys planned Tom's showing up at the last minute for the scavenger hunt? You were just trying to prove what you knew all along—that Tom and I are perfect for each other."

"If you say so," Gabrielle said with a smile.

"Yes," Alyssa added. "Whatever you say."

Megan twirled in a circle. "With Tom as my boyfriend, it will be like being on permanent vacation."

"You have to settle down sometime," Gabrielle teased.

"Why?" Megan asked. "While we were locked in that closet and then stranded out in that raft, we talked about a lot of things. And settling down in the near future wasn't one of them!"

"Whatever works," Alyssa said as she stowed her suitcase in the trunk. "College isn't for everyone."

Gabrielle and Megan turned to face her. Are you going to turn down your scholarship?" Gabrielle asked.

"I'm tired of doing what other people want me to do," Alyssa said. "I can put off accepting my scholarship for an entire year. I know it's going to be hard facing my parents and messing up their dreams for my future security, but . . ."

"But, what?" Megan asked.

"Well . . ." Alyssa hesitated. "I picked up a brochure for a cruise line, and . . . I'm thinking of applying for a job on one of their ships. I want to travel, and because I doubt that my parents will support such a 'wild' scheme . . ."

"You'll work your way around the world!" Megan sighed. "How romantic! Is Dylan going?"

Alyssa smiled softly. She raised one eyebrow. "We'll see."

Trevor came by just as they were about to leave. "I couldn't let you go without giving you this." From behind his back, he pulled out a bright yellow T-shirt with the *Party Animal* logo emblazoned in black across the front. "To remind you of me while you're back in school," he added.

Gabrielle looked down at her sleeveless, black, button-down blouse and her black, pleated shorts. Then she smiled up at Trevor and grabbed the yellow shirt from his hand.

"Just a second," she called as she ran back into the condo.

A moment later, she emerged wearing the yellow T-shirt tucked into her shorts.

Three pairs of eyes stared at her.

"Well? How do I look?" Gabrielle asked.

Megan and Alyssa smiled as Trevor took both her hands in his and looped them around his neck. "Of course you know," he said huskily just before he kissed her, "that this is going to make it *very* hard to wait until summer."

When they had parted, but were still in each other's arms, he said, "I guess this means I'll have to come visit you in a month. I wouldn't want you to forget me."

"Not a chance of that," Gabrielle said, swooping in for another kiss just as Tom and Dylan pulled up in their respective cars.

"Ready to go?" Tom asked. "I just returned the bikes Megan and I left on the road and I'm ready to roll."

Gabrielle shut the trunk of the Mustang and turned to hug Aunt Kate who had come out to say good-bye. "I can't wait until June," she said.

"I wonder why?" Kate replied with a chuckle. "I wasn't much of a chaperone," she added.

"Nonsense," Megan said. "You're the best!"

"Absolutely," Alyssa agreed.

In turn, each girl gave Kate a hug and a small token of her appreciation.

"Are you sure you won't change your mind and ride with me?" Tom asked Megan.

"And me?" Dylan added, looking at Alyssa.

"Sorry, guys." Megan put one arm around Gabrielle and the other around Alyssa. "We started this trip together . . ."

"And we're going to finish it together," Alyssa said. "Oh, no!" she exclaimed. "I'm starting to sound like Megan!"

"Could be worse," Megan quipped. "You could sound like Gabby!"

"You, my dear," Gabrielle said, "have gone too far this time. Get in the car!"

"Okay, okay!" Megan giggled and turned to the boys. "What would I do without Gabby around to keep me in line?"

With one last kiss each and one last look at the ocean, the girls drove off.

"It's been an amazing ten days," Gabrielle commented as they moved into the line of traffic heading out of Coconut Beach. "I didn't want to come to Coconut Beach in the first place, and now I'm going to spend my summer here, *and* possibly go to art school with Trevor in the fall."

"I lost my fiancé, but gained my *self*," Alyssa said.

"And I came looking for a fling, and fell in love with the boy next door," Megan said.

"Everything would have been perfect if only we'd won the scavenger hunt! Still, I think the three of us make a pretty good team," Gabrielle said. "It's good to have friends."

"True friends," Alyssa said. "Ones you can count on."

"Which brings me to my big idea," Megan said. She rummaged through her purse and pulled out a colorful brochure.

"What big idea?" Gabrielle asked warily.

"Picture this," Megan said, leaning over the front seat and opening the brochure. "The three of us, sauntering down the Champs Elyseés in Paris, boating on the Rhine River, checking out the Leaning Tower of Pisa . . ."

"What are you talking about?" Alyssa asked. "You can't mean . . . ?"

"Yes, I do mean," Megan replied. "What do you say to ten days in Europe next spring! If we work really hard and save our money, just think of the adventures we'll have over there!"

Beginning this month, a wonderful new series by Janet Quin-Harkin called FRIENDS. Join Tess and Ali, total opposites and best friends, as they spend four unforgettable summers together at the beach.

#1 *Starring Tess & Ali.*   Ali is all ready for a boring and lonely summer when she discovers a girl her own age has moved in next door. Tess is wild and wonderful, but Ali knows Tess is hiding something from her.

#2 *Tess & Ali and the Teeny Bikini.*   Tess and Ali are excited about their second summer together at the beach. Then Jasmine, a snobby friend from California, moves in with Tess, and Ali's worried that there's no room left for her in Tess's life.

#3 *Boy Trouble for Tess & Ali.*   Together for their third summer, Tess and Ali are surrounded by boys at the beach. Tess develops a crush on Ali's older brother, but Ali is the one to find a real boyfriend first, and Tess is furious.

#4 *Tess & Ali, Going on Fifteen.*   The girls share their final summer at the beach. As they weather the traumas of the summer, they wonder if their friendship will survive without the beach.

Last month we published an excerpt from Book #1 of Janet Quin Harkin's FRIENDS, *Starring Tess & Ali*.

Here's a sneak preview of what happens when Jasmine, Tess's glamorous fourteen-year-old friend from California, comes to Rose Bay for the summer in FRIENDS #2:

Tess and Ali and the Teeny Bikini

They were crossing the bridge to the island when Jasmine said to Peter, "I really like this car. It moves so well."

Peter looked pleased. "I do a lot of work on it," he said. "Want to drive?"

"Sure," Jasmine said.

Ali opened her mouth to say that Jasmine didn't have a license, but Tess nudged her. "She drives fine," Tess whispered. "I've driven with her. Besides, it's totally deserted out here. Don't worry."

Jasmine was already in the driver's seat. She clicked her seatbelt shut and released the brake. The car moved forward smoothly. Ali gradually started breathing again. Jasmine did seem to know how to drive after all, and Tess was right—

the road was deserted at this time of day. As Jasmine picked up confidence, she started to drive faster.

"Wow, this car is awesome. I want one just like it," she shouted to Peter.

"Don't miss the turn to Rose Bay," Ali warned.

The turn came up on the left, almost hidden behind a row of pine trees. Jasmine saw it at the last minute and braked hard. The next moment the wheels were sliding over the sandy surface. Jasmine screamed. Ali was frozen. Peter tried to grab the wheel.

"Steer into the skid!" he was yelling.

The world seemed to be spinning around and around in slow motion. Ali grabbed Tess and closed her eyes, waiting for the final, inevitable crash.

Suddenly she realized they weren't spinning any more. She opened her eyes. The car had come to rest beside the road, among blueberry bushes and tall ferns. Everyone breathed again.

"Phew, that was lucky," Peter said.

"I'm sorry," Jasmine muttered. "I didn't see the stupid turn until it was too late."

"It's okay. It wasn't your fault. There's a lot of

sand on the road," Peter said. "Let's just hope we can get out of this field."

"I hope I haven't scratched your car," Jasmine said.

Don't worry about it," Peter said. "Maybe I'd better drive the rest of the way." He got out of the car. "No real damage done," he called, as he climbed into the driver's seat. Very gently he eased the car, wheels protesting against the scrub and sand, back onto the road. A few minutes later, they pulled up outside Ali's house, and the three girls got out.

Jasmine waved and called to Peter, "Bye, see you tomorrow," as if nothing had happened. Tess waved, too, and Peter drove off.

Ali's legs were trembling so much they would hardly obey her. She grabbed Tess and pulled her aside. "I hope you're satisfied," she said. "Jasmine nearly got us killed!"

Tess shook her off. "Don't make such a big thing out of it," she said. "We're okay, aren't we? Nothing really happened."

"Nothing really happened?" Ali shouted. "She was risking our lives!"

"Ali, it was just a little skid," Tess said. "And we're fine. So forget about it. I'm sure Peter won't let her drive again. There's nothing to worry about."

"Oh, sure," Ali muttered. "Do you know what my parents would say if they heard about this?"

Tess glanced across at Jasmine, who was leaning against the gate post looking bored. She winced as if she was embarrassed by Ali's outburst. "Come on, Al," Tess whispered. "Calm down, okay?"

"You want me to calm down?" Ali shouted. "Oh, I'm just so uncool because I don't pretend I'm eighteen and crash cars."

Tess glanced at Jasmine again. Jasmine was examining her fingernails.

"What's the matter with you this summer? You're no fun anymore," Tess said. "You're either worrying or you're sulking."

"No fun anymore?" Ali shouted even louder now. "Is that your idea of fun—nearly flipping over in a car?"

"It didn't nearly flip over. It turned around a couple of times," Tess said, shrugging her shoulders and sticking her hands into the pockets of her shorts.

"Come on, Tess, I want to get home and take a shower," Jasmine called impatiently.

Ali longed to take Tess and shake her. *Stop acting like this! Stop pretending you're Jasmine and be the way you really are,* she wanted to shout. But she knew it was useless.

"Okay," Ali said in what she hoped was a calm voice. "Maybe I'm just immature, but I don't want to hang around Jasmine anymore. I guess you can't be friends with both of us."

Tess opened her mouth in surprise. "Hey, Al, you don't mean that, do you?"

"Sure, I do."

Tess hesitated. Ali could see her trying to decide what to do next. She drew in the sand with her toes. "Look, Al, she's my guest," Tess said.

"Fine," Ali said, and she heard her voice quiver. "But I'm through tagging along with the two of you."

She turned and hurried into the house before she started to cry.

**Enter the FRIENDS Phone Giveaway and
Ultimate Pen Pal Match-up!**

WIN A PAIR OF PHONES!

One for you, one for your friend

100 Grand Prizes—   The first 100 respondents receive a pair of FRIENDS phones.

500 First Prizes—   The next 500 respondents win *Homecoming*, Book #1 in Janet Quin-Harkin's SENIOR YEAR series, coming in October 1991 from HarperPaperbacks.

EVERYONE GETS A FRIENDS PEN PAL!

See FRIENDS #1, *Starring Tess & Ali*.

ON SALE NOW